THE
EYES
OF THE
WIND

He had seen her in his dreams.

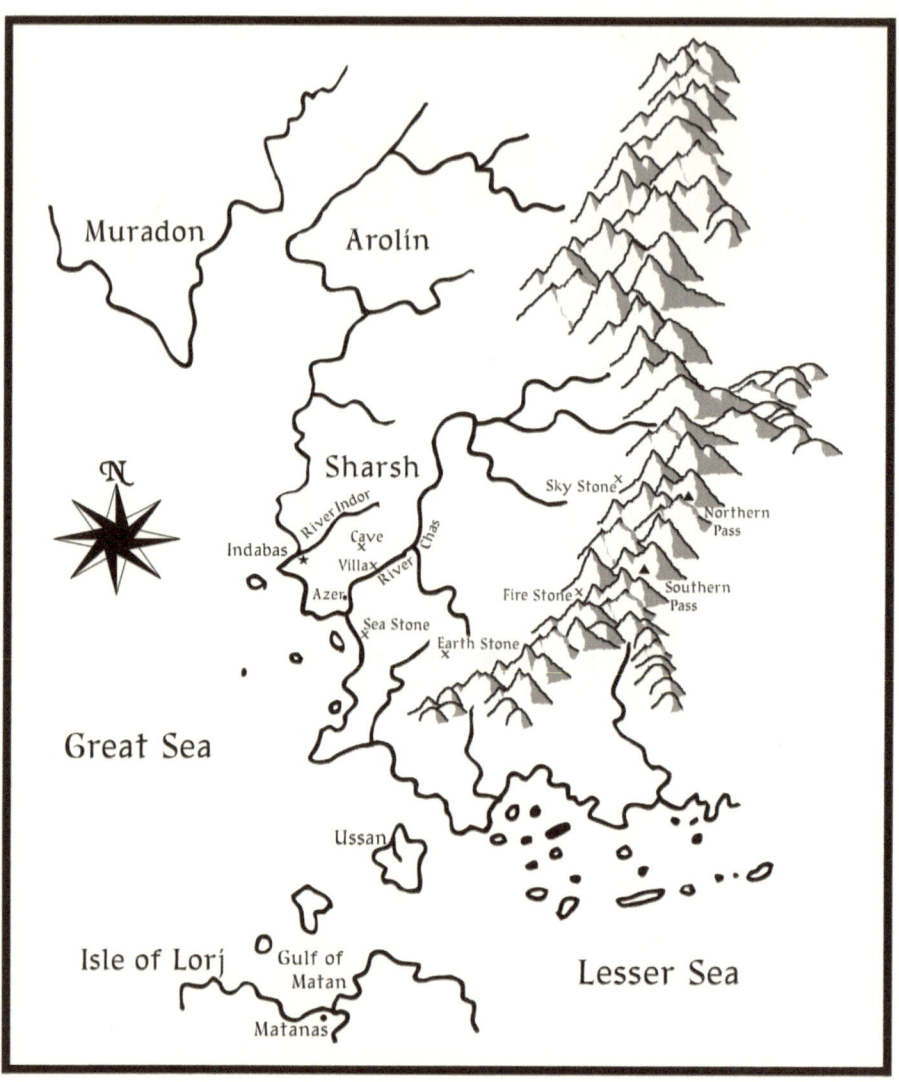

Sharsh
at the time of Saj the Seer

THE EYES OF THE WIND

Stephen Brooke

Arachis Press 2016

The Eyes of the Wind
©2016 Stephen Brooke

ISBN 978-1-937745-33-2

Arachis Press
4803 Peanut Road
Graceville, FL 32440
http://arachispress.com

Setting I.
SETTING FORTH

1.

"My mother had the second sight," said the young man, gazing toward the distant coast.

His companion raised an eyebrow. Only the one, for a great scar crossing his forehead and left cheekbone made the other immobile. "I thought you were skeptical of such things, Master Saj."

"I am skeptical of things I have not seen with my own eyes," came the reply. Those eyes, when he turned them to the captain, were gray, the deep gray of thunderstorms. Looking back to the east, he continued, "And now I see land. That's Arolin, isn't it?" The distant coast could barely be made out, little more than a haze on the horizon.

"We're already past Arolin. I took a more southerly course rather than cross the Gulf and hang close to the coast." The sailor nodded in the direction of the land. "That be Sharsh."

Saj nodded absently. "Mother said I would make my fortune in a far land."

"'Tis not that far to Sharsh, my lad."

"I suppose not," came the grave reply. "But it would have seemed very far to her."

Must be dead, thought Captain Sokor. As far as he had known, his young supercargo had no family. The sail flapped above him. Good, the men on the steering oar were already compensating for the wind shift. "We should make Indabas in good time if this breeze holds."

"I hear they have a new kind of sail in the south, that allows one to sail into the wind."

The captain spat over the railing. "Oh, aye, I've heard that too.

And like you, my boy, I am skeptical of things I have not seen with my own eyes."

"Some see with other eyes, sir." Saj returned his gaze to the distant coastline. "Some see with the eyes of dream."

Sokor saw no need to respond. "Two days should find us safe in port," he said, then thought on that. "Three, anyway. If the winds hold steady."

"They usually do, this time of year, no?" It was spring, and spring was a good time to voyage.

"Steady enough," spoke the captain, "but a wind that is favorable for trade is favorable for pirates as well. I heard reports of ships lurking about the mouth of the Chas, before we left port."

"South of where we are headed, isn't it?"

"Aye. But ships have a way of moving about."

~

Fog came with the dawn, and a fickle breeze. Saj had dreamed troubling dreams during the night, tossing on his thin and narrow pallet spread on the deck, and arose early to stand peering out at the sea. He knew to pay attention to his dreams.

A far land, he thought, that was what Mother said. He had not seen that far land himself; it was difficult to glimpse ones own future, maybe even impossible. Could it be Sharsh? There were Muram colonies as far south as the great island of Lorj now, ever since the explorer Matan had sailed there a couple of generations earlier.

Perhaps that would be his destination and his destiny. Saj shrugged. He would find out eventually. What was that, there on the mist-shrouded horizon?

He strained to make it out for a few seconds. "Captain Sokor!" he called. As the sailor turned to him from his place by the steering oar, Saj pointed toward what was now identifiable as a ship. No, two ships.

Sokor gazed out at them for a moment and scowled. "Black sails," was all he said, before looking to his own sail. "We'll need more of a breeze to outrun yon galleys."

Black sails. Saj knew well what those signified. He had heard tales of such all his young life. The men on those galleys were pirates from the old Muram kingdoms beyond the sea. If they took this ship, there would be no mercy — it might be better to die at their hands than to be sold into slavery.

Or be chained in a galley, rowing in pursuit of more victims for their implacable masters. Saj very much hoped his mother had seen his future correctly. The sun was burning through the fog now, making those black sails and the long black hulls beneath them fully visible, and with the sun came wind.

"Pirates, most definitely," said Sokor. "I thank all the gods of Sharsh and the Mura for this wind. Aye, and the goddesses too. Keep her steady!" he called to the steersmen, as calmly as though guiding his ship into a mooring. To young Saj, he said, "We must stay beyond bow shot and hope they have no weapons with a greater range."

"I know I will not die here," replied Saj, not at all so certain of this in his heart.

"Maybe not, lad, but that doesn't mean the rest of us can't." He glanced toward their pursuers and then back to Saj. "Can you shoot? We have bows."

"I'm better with a sling. I'll get mine." Saj rummaged through his duffel, a small woven bag that contained all he owned in the world, and pulled the weapon forth. "I've only a few pellets."

"There should be enough usable pebbles in our ballast. You know where that is," said Sokor and turned back to the business of outrunning the pirate craft. The younger man hurried down a ladder into the hold. Yes, there were bits of rock among the ballast that could be employed — not ideal, mind you, but certainly better than having nothing to hurl at their enemy. Saj filled a pouch and scrambled back to the deck.

The captain was in conference with his mate. "The seas are growing, Captain," observed the man. "That should make rowing harder for them." Saj gazed toward the bobbing vessels following them. Yes, he could see how the waves would make things more difficult. The twin banks of oars sometimes missed the water altogether on their strokes. They might outrun them yet.

But the galleys were swift, even propelled solely by wind, their long, narrow hulls built for speed. The broad cargo ship of Captain Sokor, however, was crafted for sailing and could certainly turn more sharply than its adversaries.

"I see no catapults," reported the mate, scanning the still-distant pirate vessels. "That might be a spanker in the bow of the closer ship."

"No more range than a bow, if as much," answered Sokor. "If they get close, it could do damage."

They would certainly rather capture us undamaged, felt Saj.

~

An hour passed, and another. Neither pursuers nor pursued could make much difference in the gap that lay between them. Weapons had been passed out to Sokor's crew, only a handful of men, truly, but ready to fight. Bows, spears, swords — Saj himself took a short, heavy-bladed sword, the sort used by Sharshite infantry. That would not require as much of the finesse and training that the young Mur lacked.

"'Tis long till sunset," observed the captain. "Yet if we can manage to stay ahead of them until then, we may be safe and see Indabas on the morrow." He looked across the waters. "We need to turn back to the east some or we won't see Indabas at all."

"That can be dangerous, sir," warned the mate.

"Aye, it might let them gain on us. Not yet."

But, eventually, they must. Sokor knew this, the mate knew this. Maybe those pirates over there knew it too. When the captain finally chose to come around, under a clear noon sky, a cry arose from the pirates, hoping at last to close on their prey.

A rain of arrows. Most fell short but a few clattered weakly, spent, on the deck. The enemy was still too distant to do damage with their bows.

And the opposite, of course, was true, though the sailors chafed to return fire. The leather thongs of Saj's sling dangled from his hand.

That, too, was of no use at this distance. Indeed, it had not the range of the bows but could be deadly if the enemy drew closer.

The two galleys had spread apart, perhaps hoping to capture their quarry between them, if it again turned one way or another. That would not be necessary, Sokor knew, if the brisk wind held steady — he could run before it all day.

Best though, that it not grow too strong. Those heavier galleys would benefit from that. His vessel could outrun them as it blew now. The seas continued to be heavy, also to his advantage, with a swell rolling out of the northwest. Storms coming off the coasts of Clisidon, a late-season incursion of arctic air, could bring such waves.

"Those waves will be breaking on the bar at Indor-mouth," Sokor muttered, mostly to himself. "It may not be the easiest passage." If they reached it.

~

The wind had gradually become more easterly and less suitable for Sokor's chosen course. He wished that he had one of those new sails of which young Saj had spoken, the ones that would allow one to sail into the wind, or at least close to it. It was said that they were triangular in shape. The captain again prayed to the gods of both Muradon and Sharsh that he would have a chance to see one, someday.

Still, he was managing to keep beyond reach of his adversaries' arrows. Surely those Mura would give up eventually — there would be no profit in continuing the pursuit over-long. Now they seemed to be laying onto the oars, despite the rough surf. He could imagine the whip-driven rowers below the galley decks, straining to keep up the pace their masters demanded. And he would need to adjust his course again shortly. Headlands could be seen distantly to the east, ones he recognized as lying not far to the north of the Indor valley. It would not do to draw too close to those treacherous cliffs.

The ship wallowed as a sudden shift in the wind caught them unaware. One galley drew close to their starboard, too close. More arrows. A man fell with a shaft through his body. That was certainly a lucky shot, felt Sokor; the pirates could not be aiming at anyone in particular and even if they were, the bucking decks would not permit any sort of accuracy.

Then they used the spanker. This device, as a weapon, was simplicity itself. A springy board was bent far back and then released to impact a heavy spear or bolt and send it flying. Close up, such a missile could strike with considerable force. Undoubtedly, the pirates would attempt to damage them at the waterline.

The first attempt was too low, and skipped off the waves, to slam into the ship sideways, doing no harm. Arrows continued to fly, from both ships now, as Sokor struggled to bring his vessel around and escape. Damn this clumsy steering oar!

Another bolt flew and this one struck fully, but a bit high, crashing through the ship's side a few feet above the water. Now the wind was in his sails and Sokor turned the stern of his ship to the Muram pirates. They would not be able to come around so quickly and pursue. So he wanted to believe, anyway.

The captain's belief was justified. The pirate vessel again fell behind them, although the other ship made an effort to cut across their path. A few arrows flew from its decks and then it, too, was beyond range.

The galleys remained so until night hid them from sight.

~

A lantern was held high. "If the seas weren't so high, this wouldn't be much of a problem," the mate said. Seawater sloshed into the hold through a ragged breach in the ship's side. Saj picked up what remained of the missile that had made that hole, a thick splintered wooden shaft with nothing more than a sharpened end — a primitive yet effective weapon.

"Patch it as best you can," ordered Captain Sokor. "I know it will leak but we can try to limit it. And get a couple men down here to start bailing."

"I'll board it up," Saj offered. "I know something of carpentry." It had, indeed, been the family business until his father's untimely death. Had it not been for that seeming misfortune, he suspected that he would be back home still, hammering and sawing, rather than being out in the world to make his fortune. Yes, he would be making his fortune — of this he was more certain than ever.

Why else had he escaped danger? Oh, yes, here was another danger, a ship threatening to sink beneath him, but he was equally certain he would come out of it safely. Something waited for him ahead, something important. He believed this. He *knew* this.

Canvas, tar, boards — the breach, as wide as the thickness of a man's body, was covered over. No, it was not completely waterproof and, no, it would certainly not last long as a repair. Saj, and the crew, could only hope that it would hold until they reached the docks of Indabas.

Dawn showed them a sea free of pirates. It also showed a high headland rising directly ahead of them.

"We're too far south! That be Citadel Point," said the mate.

Sokor scowled. "They need a lighthouse out there!"

Saj could see that some sort of fortress was built on the heights, over toward the east, undoubtedly the reason for the name. That would be the Viceroy's headquarters, from which the Mura administered all of Sharsh. All of Sharsh they controlled, that is — there were areas in the south and east where their hold was tenuous, places where there was no Muram presence at all.

"We can bring her around," stated Captain Sokor. He sounded sure but Saj doubted he was. "Damn these waves!"

"We'll have to go broadside into them," whispered the mate. He mumbled something to himself that was most certainly a prayer. The waves could be seen breaking in shallow, rock-riddled water that lay far too close to their vessel. They would need to turn toward those rocks to bring it around.

The ship listed crazily, rocked by the waves, but managed to turn onto the desired course. A light breeze blew in an opportune direction and, too, it seemed there was a bit of current that favored their progress.

Then, a scrape, a groan from the hull. "I think your repairs have given way, Master Saj. Let us pray that they lasted long enough," said

11

Sokor. "Here is our passage into the river." He regarded the waves breaking on the shallow sandbar before them. "The tide is low but we must chance it, or sink within sight of our safe harbor."

He looked upward, ascertaining that the sail was as it should be, then went aft and took the steering oar himself. "Hold on!" he called, turning his ship, sending it speeding forward. A wave lifted them over the bar and into the River Indor. Sokor nodded his head in satisfaction. "We should tie up at the docks within half an hour," he announced.

2.

"Keep the sword, my boy. You may need it where you go."

"Thank you, Captain." Saj turned to the array of goods stacked high on the dock. "It is fortunate there wasn't much damage to our cargo. You'll need to pull the ship out for repairs now, won't you?"

"Aye. But the owners' agent here will have to approve it first. I thank you, young sir, for going below and patching things up again. Otherwise, she might be on the bottom of the river."

"That agent should have been her by now. We both need to get on with things."

Saj nodded, somewhat distractedly, and turned toward the pile of cargo. "I suppose I could start sorting it out."

"There are fellows here paid to do that, lad. But you'll want to keep an eye on them while they're at it. Ah, here's the man now!"

A tall but stooped man of lugubrious mien, wrapped in a reasonably clean white Sharshite toga, strode toward them, his secretary scurrying behind him. "Captain Sokor!" he called, in a cheerful voice that did not at all seem to fit his appearance. "I hear you had a close escape."

"Greetings to you, Master Vasale. We did indeed have a little trouble with pirates."

"Ah, Sokor, you have too much modesty. I shall certainly write a glowing report to our employers." He turned to the younger man. "You must be Saj. My greeting to you as well, young sir. I would commend you to them, too, but I understand you will be leaving their service."

"As soon as I deliver the goods with which I was entrusted," replied the Mur, gesturing broadly toward the cargo. "We shall need to sort it out, first. There was a hurry to get it out of the hold."

The Sharshite nodded his head. "Understood. I'll have some men down here shortly. Paxo, here," he indicated his secretary, "will stay and help with the inventory.

"Come on to my office, Sokor, and we'll get our end of the business sorted out." He turned and hurried away. The captain followed at a more leisurely pace.

Paxo was a small, olive-skinned man with an accent Saj did not recognize. He did, however, have suspicions as to his origin. "Are you from Lorj, Master Paxo?" he inquired. "Think me not rude for asking. I'm considering heading there."

The man smiled broadly. "All I ever wanted was to leave, sir. I like it much better here, even if it does get too cold." He cocked his head at Saj. "But you're thinking of setting up on your own, aren't you? Lots of opportunities for that down there. I myself was happy just for the chance to attach myself to a successful man like Vasale." He chuckled softly. "I like certainty in my life."

A trio of burly stevedores joined them shortly and the various crates and bundles were satisfactorily sorted and carried off to the proper warehouses. Saj would have a couple days before he needed to be on the road, delivering goods to various villages and manors in the interior. Most of the other items carried by Sokor's ship would be sold right here in Indabas.

That was none of Saj's business, though all business interested him.

~

"We'll be pulling the old girl out tomorrow," Captain Sokor informed him. "And you will be on the road. I reckon we shall see no more of you, Master Saj."

"He will need to stop back by here to collect his pay," said Vasale. "Where then, boy?"

"I am thinking Lorj. Maybe I shall take ship to Matanas."

"Ah. You'll have to find some of those three-cornered sails for me down there," said the captain. "Before the pirates start using them!" He drank deeply from his cup of wine. Sharsh was noted for its many good wines; some even said a desire for them had first led to the Muram invasion. Set it off, maybe, thought Saj, but the causes would be much deeper and more complex than that.

"Once you travel around my homeland a bit, you may find you like it right here," spoke Vasale. He held up a hand to attract the barman. "Another jug, if you will, sir!"

14

Sokor leaned forward and spoke earnestly. "Not everyone here is fond of our people, Saj, and you look about as Muram as anyone I've ever seen on this side of the Great Sea. Be cautious, lad."

This was true, thought Saj. His black hair, hawk-like nose, high cheekbones, all spoke of the adventurers who had crossed the water to found their empire. Admittedly, that dark hair was somewhat curly rather than straight, but even in the old kingdoms of the Mura, beyond the sea, pure blood, the blood of the nomadic tribes that had come from the vast interior, was rare.

There might be war again in those kingdoms and the emperor might or might not send ships and men. That was no matter to the young traveler — he intended to make his fortune elsewhere.

"Good advice," said Vasale. Lowering his voice, he continued. "I hear you may, ah, have the second sight."

Saj glanced at Sokor. The man had obviously been talking, though he kept a straight face now. "I may have a gift of sorts, sir. It does — it does give me some, shall we say, advantages in business. So I don't speak of it."

"Wise," agreed the Sharshite. "Neither would I," he said and dropped the subject. "What think you of our city?"

"It looks so different from the towns back home! It is a new city, isn't it?"

"That it is. There was only a small fishing village standing here a century ago. We Sharshites tended to turn inward, into our own land, rather than toward the sea and all our large towns were well away from the coast. But the Mura decided to place their capital here and built Indabas."

'Indabas,' Saj recognized, was a sort of bastardized name, cobbled together from Muram and Sharshic usage. "It does not look like the Mura built it." It most certainly did not resemble the collections of blocky houses, constructed of rough-hewn timber, that made up most towns in his homeland.

"The forts do," said Sokor.

Vasale nodded. "That is true. Of course, the town itself was built by Sharshites. It doesn't look much different from what you'll see trav-

15

eling inland. I do think this is the largest city in the land, now. For all I know, it might be the largest city in the world."

"They say Tesra is bigger," Sokor told him. "Not that I've ever seen it."

"Didn't your ancestors sack it?" asked the Sharshite.

"Relatives, anyway," admitted the sailor.

~

Saj was not a large man. He felt even smaller in the streets of Indabas. The capital of Muram-ruled Sharsh was indeed a large city, and the most important center of commerce on either side of the Great Sea.

There were five large wagons loaded with the goods he need deliver, each pulled by a team of oxen. The young Mur felt almost overwhelmed by the responsibility.

Almost, but not quite. Saj had a great deal of faith in his abilities. He saw himself as a practical man, a man of the world, a skeptic who trusted only in himself and had no need for the gods. Yet, he could not deny the strange and inexplicable gift he possessed, the one he had inherited from his mother.

The architecture here was very different from his home. The houses were long, and low built, rarely more than two stories. Typically, at least in the business districts, there would be a taller central section with a lower, single-story area on either side, containing offices, shops, and so on. There were rounded arches everywhere.

Further from the main way, he knew, there were taller tenements and, beyond those, the hovels that would appear on the outskirts of any city. These he had only glimpsed as he had gone about his business, preparing for his journey into the heart of Sharsh. Up the Indor he would go or, more properly, he would parallel the river, turning aside here and there to deliver items that had been ordered from Muradon. There was a good highway, he was told.

What might the nobles and the wealthy of Sharsh wish to have brought to them from the Muram homeland? There was cloth, yes, mostly linen but also wool. Sheep outnumbered humans back home,

16

Saj was sure. There was lace; that seemed a luxury here though common in Muradon. Both men and women would employ the dark winter days in its making, the long hours spent shut indoors. Metal work, mostly of the more ornate sort. Certain precious stones, especially amber. A surprising amount of his cargo seemed related to horses — tack of various kinds, including saddles both practical and ornamental. Sharsh had not been a country of horsemen before the Muram conquest, but that was changing.

Saj chose to ride in the final wagon, so he might readily keep an eye on his entire convoy. Slowly they progressed up the wide cobblestone thoroughfare that led to the tall northern city gates and out into the country.

3.

The towns of Sharsh did indeed look rather like Indabas. The style of the buildings was much the same, the ubiquitous arches, the stuccoed walls. Here they tended to be even lower built, however, rarely more than one story. The nobles lived not in castles but in villas. Not at all defensible, thought Saj, though generally quite practical in their layouts. Sharsh had long been at peace and was rather decentralized; it had proven quite unready when the Mura invaded.

It was a pleasant, attractive country to travel through, along the well-maintained, tree-lined roads, but not a place for Saj to settle. There might be more opportunity here than back in his homeland with its rather rigid caste system, but not much more. One by one, the wains were emptied and sent home with their drivers.

"We must cross the hills now for the final delivery," he was told by Bawaith, his final driver in his final, half-loaded wagon. "Sarowhem is on the River Chas."

Saj had picked up enough Sharshic to know 'whem' meant something like 'farm' or 'manor.' Several of the estates they had visited had names that ended that way. As to what 'Saro' signified, he neither knew nor cared, but suspected it to be a family name. "I hear it is a larger river than Indor."

"Much larger. And longer — it runs all the way from the mountains."

"I suppose we are still far from those mountains. I would have liked to have seen them before heading back."

"I was there once," said the man. "It is wild country, empty country." He grinned. "You would find no Muram soldiers to protect you." Companies of those soldiers had occasionally passed them on their journey.

"Then there is no profit to be made visiting them," decided Saj.

"Your soul might profit," came Bawaith's rejoinder. "The hills between the rivers are low and there are good roads. It should be an easy way. But," he added, "there is an area of ill repute we might wish to skirt."

"Bandits?" asked the Mur.

"Evil spirits. Ghosts. Or so it is said. There is a cave that most avoid." He shrugged. "As far as bandits go, you are more likely to encounter them in the valley of the Chas. Muram authority is not so strong there, on the edge of the areas they control."

"Then I would just as soon get there quickly and get away again. We shall travel past this cave if it is the shorter route."

~

There were eyes, glowing in the dark. Red. Blue. Green. Gold. So did Saj dream that night, in the hills above Sarowhem. He could make nothing of the dream. He spoke little to Bawaith as they prepared to break camp.

Late morning brought them across the highest part of their road, which began a leisurely descent toward the River Chas. Could Saj make out that river in the distance or was it just an illusion, a shimmer of the air? The valley they had entered was broad, that was certain, and apparently not as populous as that of the Indor.

A hand on his arm. He turned to Bawaith, who pointed toward the hillside above them, to the right of the road. A low cliff began about halfway up that hill and in that cliff was an opening. "Your cave?" he asked.

"Not mine, sir!" The driver chuckled and cracked his whip above the four stolid oxen drawing their wain. It would not hurry them, Saj knew, but he sensed that the man was uncomfortable here and wanted past the cave as soon as possible. He stared up at that opening.

"I must go in," he told Bawaith. Yes, he realized that now. The cave was tied to his dream. "Go on down the road as far as you feel comfortable and await me." He jumped to the ground and then, looking up to the driver, he added, "Hand me down my sword, will you? It might not be a bad idea to carry it."

"Not a bad idea at all, sir," agreed Bawaith. "But it is a bad idea to go in there." His gaze went to the dark hole in the cliff. "Why?"

"I have seen it," was Saj's only reply. He watched the wagon trundle on southward before turning to his destination.

19

He climbed toward the cave. There was an obvious pathway, so, it would seem, not all avoided the place. In few minutes, he stood before the opening, half again as high as a man and as wide as four abreast. He turned and looked down at the road. Bawaith and the wagon were disappearing over a rise.

A sound behind him. Tall grotesque creatures stood there, staring down at him.

~

"I am most sorry if our masks startled you," apologized the High Priest. "They are part of our rituals." He added, in a lower voice, "We knew someone was to come but we did not expect you right then. We — did not see you."

Perhaps these priests had some abilities similar to his own, thought Saj. He looked about the torch-lit cavern. This space had been enlarged by human hands, hadn't it? There were perhaps a dozen of the saffron-robed priests, all men, present.

Their robes might be of a pale yellow but their skins were black. Saj had seen a number of such men at the port of Indabas, some from Lorj, some from further south, from islands he could not name, and now he could recognize their Baxac accent. "This seems an odd place for a, uh, temple," said Saj.

"More a shrine," came the reply. "And it is a place of power. But we came here because we expected your arrival."

"Me? I am no more than a delivery boy on my rounds. And I have nothing in my wagon for you."

"You are Saj the Seer," the priest gravely stated. "You have been foretold."

Saj did not at all like the sound of that.

"I am named Kambak," continued the man. "I serve Munu. All of us here serve Munu."

"Munu? A Baxac god?" Saj knew little of the people of the south. Far too little, he told himself. Lack of knowledge ever would put one at a disadvantage.

"Munu is the all-encompassing god-force who fills all things. So, not exactly a god," replied Kambak.

"The spirit of existence," offered another priest, who had remained unobtrusively at the High Priest's elbow.

"Yes, quite," agreed Kambak. They stopped before a golden statue, a stylized depiction of four man-like beings — Saj felt that two were probably meant to be female — melded into one. Each head faced a different direction and in each head was a single empty eye-socket.

The High Priest gazed upon it for a few moments before speaking. "This does not depict Munu but some god of the Ildin." Kambak's tone was dismissive, contemptuous even.

"Banat," said a dark diminutive man who had already been standing before the image. "The Father of the Winds in their pantheon."

"Oh, yes, that is right, Xit. And lord of the elements, isn't he?" The High Priest went on with his speech. "The statue is of no importance. It is but a lump of metal. It is the missing eyes that matter. They are the Jewels of the Elements, the Eyes of the Wind."

~

"All that is known for certain is that the jewels were stolen by Im, the infamous wizard-thief, centuries ago."

"In the south," added Kambak's second, who had remained a mostly-silent presence.

"Yes, the statue was in in a temple of Banat, then, somewhat south of here. Ildin folk dwelt there in those days, not Sharshites." The High Priest picked up his cup and soberly regarded it before replacing it on the table. "How the stones came to be scattered after that, no one seems to know. We do know that they were not scattered too far. The gems are in this land, more or less. We can sense their power but not their exact locations."

Saj began to understand. "You think I can find them."

"Not exactly, my young guest. We *know* you can find them."

The torchlight flickered on the sandstone walls. They were seated at one side of the cavern; apparently, this one large space was all there

21

was to the cave and the priests slept, ate, and worshiped here. "And what is in it for me?" asked the Mur. It was the obvious question so he might as well get to it.

"We will reward you as we are able," spoke Kambak. "We, admittedly, have taken a vow of poverty."

That did not sound promising to Saj, but the aide spoke up. "The statue, your holiness."

"Oh, yes, of course," the High Priest said. "We have no use for the image of that heathen god. Solid gold and all yours if you gather the Eyes for us."

Saj turned his eyes to the statue. That would be worth quite a bit wouldn't it? But how could he be sure it would be given to him if he succeeded? For that matter, how would he transport that weighty piece of metal?

Weighty — if it were indeed solid gold. For all he knew, it might be hollow. And only gilded.

"I am willing to tell you where they are, if I can indeed sense them, but I'll not be the one to go after them. I have business elsewhere," averred the young man.

The two priests gave each other a knowing look, barely noticeable. "This is not unexpected, Master Saj," said Kambak. "Very well, you may continue on your way with our blessings. Remember, though, our offer and know that we can be of assistance to you in many things."

"Many things, indeed," added the other priest.

4.

The wagon was waiting no more than half a league down the road, the embers of a fire still glowing beside it in the early morning. The driver looked up from his breakfast as Saj approached.

"If you hadn't shown up by tomorrow morning, I would have gone on and made the delivery myself," Bawaith told him. He asked nothing of Saj's doings and Saj was grateful for that.

"Anything left?" he asked, crouching beside the man.

"Nothing hot," replied Bawaith. "Would you like me to heat something up?"

"No, I'll take my breakfast cold and on the road. Let's get ourselves going."

The oxen were harnessed and soon the pair were headed down out of the hills. There was heavy forest on the slopes around them. "What sort of place is this Sarowhem?" asked Saj.

"Never been there, sir," came the answer. "But I hear the family are pretty important nobles, with large holdings." He turned his head toward his companion. "Strong allies of your people in this part of the country."

"That doesn't matter much to me. I just want to make delivery and get paid." Yet Saj had a feeling that there was some — *event* in his near future. There was something for him here, something important. What that might be, he had no inkling.

A bearded, kilt-clad woodcutter informed them that their road would lead them directly to the villa of Sarowhem. "You can't miss it, Masters," he told them. Or so Bawaith translated his words, for Saj had little understanding of Sharshic. He hoped that would not present a problem at their destination — most of the upper-class Sharshites spoke Muram but who knew how things were out here near the borders?

He felt of his stubbly chin. Perhaps he should shave and render himself more presentable before making an appearance. They wouldn't get there for a day or two anyway, so he had time to attend to that.

~

A low wall surrounded the villa of Thegn Hurrum, the Lord of Sarowhem. That would not keep anyone out, thought Saj, not anyone at all determined. Hurrum's title, he knew, was of old Sharshic origin, older even than those used during the reign of the last Sharshite dynasty. Those titles had been abolished by the Muram rulers but 'thegn' was considered fitting for those who were willing to serve the new regime.

I am presentable enough, he told himself. Freshly shaven that morning, he was clad in a reasonably clean white tunic, a gray cloak casually draped over one shoulder. Not exactly a Sharshite toga but it would do.

Hurrum did not wear a toga, either. Perhaps such formal wear was not so common out here in the country. The man was in a serviceable knee-length tunic, only a faded red stripe around its hem indicating that he was a person of high rank. Most of those about him wore kilts; that seemed to be the common garment here.

Saj had been a bit surprised to find a party waiting for him at the villa gates, the thegn among them, eager to get at his cargo. He reminded himself that this manor was far from Indabas, far from the center of things in Sharsh. Any contact with the outside would be something of an occasion.

The thegn was tall and what remained of his hair was graying. He raised a hand in greeting. "Welcome, guests, to the halls of Sarowhem." Formalities attended to, he rushed on. "Have you my new saddle in there?"

Saj was pleased that the nobleman spoke Muram to him. He hopped down from his seat and gave this Sharshite a bow. "We do indeed, my lord." He swept an arm toward the wain. "Everything here is for Sarowhem and ready to unload."

"Excellent! Belema, come on!" He turned back to Saj. "My wife, the Lady Belema."

Saj likewise gave a little bow to the Lady Belema, who seemed as eager as her husband to get at the contents of his wagon. She was accompanied by a rather tall, broad-shouldered young woman. Saj looked upon her and he knew this was what he had been destined to find in this place.

~

He had seen her in his dreams. Saj realized this now. That in itself meant nothing, of course. He tried not to stare at her across the table.

"What is wrong with you, Marana?" asked Lady Belema. "You have barely touched your dinner."

The girl gave a quick glance in Saj's direction before replying to her mother. "Oh, I was only thinking of what we might do with that new cloth."

"It will make a fine wedding gown," spoke the thegn. "Lord Gawif will be proud of his bride."

The young woman's expression did not convey enthusiasm. "Yes, Father," she murmured, and her eyes again briefly fixed on Saj.

She is tall, isn't she? he thought. Taller than I am? And she looks more like she was built to wield a battleaxe than a seamstress' needle. A descendant of fighting men — that's what she was, and he suspected she might have the heart of one.

But handsome, in her way, she was. The deep brown, almost black, hair was uncommon among her people, though Saj suspected Thegn Hurrum's locks were once of that hue. It was pulled back rather severely into practical braids that framed the strong cheekbones beneath her sky-blue eyes.

He would have to find a way to speak with the young Lady Marana. Saj knew little of what might be permitted in the home of a noble of Sharsh. They were more casual than his own people about such things, the interaction of aristocrat and commoner, he had always heard, yet more straitlaced in their relationships between the sexes.

The talk turned to the material he had brought, and what the latest styles might be for the dresses they hoped to make. The thegn listened without a great deal of interest for a time, allowing his wife and daughter to take the conversation where they would.

Eventually, the conversation came around to the saddle Saj had delivered. Marana showed more interest in this than in her future wedding gown. "I wish you had ordered a fighting saddle as well, Father," she stated. "But at least it does have stirrups."

"You know a well-bred lady should ride sidesaddle," scolded her mother.

Marana made a face at that, but did not answer.

"Stirrups — yes," said Hurrum. "There are those who still will not use them, yet they are one of the things that gave the Mura an advantage over us."

"We already had stirrups, Father," spoke Maranna. "But the Mura figured out how to best use them."

"That is true. The mounted Muram lancer was able to crash through the shield walls on which we had so long relied." He spoke to Saj. "Do you have fighting experience, young man?"

Best to be honest. "No, sir, I am no more than a merchant and a man of peace."

"In this part of the world it is difficult to be both. Things are often unsettled here."

"Your driver says you intend to go to Lorj," said Lady Belema. She had gossiped quite some time with Bawaith during the unloading of the wagon, eager to hear any news.

"It is one possibility, my lady."

"Isn't it terribly hot there?" asked Marana. "It can be bad enough here in the summers."

Saj smiled. "I won't know unless I travel there, my lady. I have heard it is pleasant enough if one remains on the coast."

"Which is where a merchant can make his fortune, eh?" Thegn Hurrum chuckled. "I wish you luck, young fellow." He rose and stretched. "I'm going to the stables. Yes, Marana, I am going to give the new saddle a closer look while I am at it."

"I'll go with you, Father. You should come too, Master Saj."

The Lady Belama looked from one to another of the trio, and gave them a wan smile. "Left alone again while they discuss horses. This happens many evenings here, Master Saj."

~

Marana dropped back from her father to walk at Saj's side. "You are going to take me away from here," she stated. "I have prayed to Esefa for this."

Saj, for a moment, thought to object. But it was what was going to happen, wasn't it? He had known that from the moment he laid eyes on the young noblewoman.

"How?" he asked, ever practical.

"Hide me in your wagon." She continued, rather vehemently, "I will not be married to that old lecher!"

The stables were roomy, and well-kept. "I do not think I have ever seen so clean a barn, my lord," said Saj, "nor one so adorned." There were even mosaics on the floors and walls, as in the villa itself.

"All of this is very old," replied the thegn. "From the days when Sharsh was powerful and we were rich. Things are not as they once were."

"Are they ever, Father?" asked Maranna.

5.

"Who is that following us?" wondered Bawaith.

Saj had his suspicions. He stood up and looked into the distance. Mounted men, riding up the road after them. And was that the baying of hounds?

"We might as well stop and let them catch up," he told the driver. Was there time to get Marana out from under the empty crates and canvas and away from the road? No, she would be spotted now. Saj sighed and waited.

In a few minutes, the wain was surrounded by mounted men and howling dogs. All those dogs seemed to focus their attention on the wagon. A man at arms leaped into it and pulled back the canvas to reveal the hidden Marana. She rose with considerable dignity to face her father.

Who seethed with anger. "You would steal my daughter, Muram dog?" Apparently Hurrum did not care for the Mura as much as his politics suggested.

Marana spoke up immediately. "No, Father, no, they did not know I had hidden myself away. I — you know well I do not want to marry Gawif." She gave Saj a somewhat contemptuous look. "These merchants were merely convenient to my plans."

The thegn looked from her to Saj and Bawaith, and then back to his daughter. Did he believe her? "Hmm. I shall take my daughter's word for this, Master Saj. Indeed, I shall apologize for her actions. Had it been otherwise, I would have set my pack upon you." He regarded the young man sternly. "But I warn you, should you ever return, that is exactly what I shall do.

"Mount up, girl. We shall speak further of this when we return home." A saddled horse was brought forward for her. Hurrum wheeled his own mount and started away. Saj noted that he was using his new saddle.

"I am glad that you had nothing to do with that," spoke Bawaith when the horsemen had disappeared into the dust and distance. His tone suggested that he had doubts of Saj's innocence.

"It was my doing, I shall admit," replied the Mur, deciding honesty would be the best idea. "I am sorry that you were placed in danger."

"Your doing? I know you rather well by now, Master Saj. You might have gone along with it but I do not think you would come up with such a plot." He cracked his whip over the heads of the oxen and they moved forward.

"His daughter is all the thegn has now. Lady Belema told me their only son was lost at sea some three years ago."

"Then she is even more of a prize for this Lord Gawif," mused Saj. "An heiress."

"No one for the likes of you and me, my friend."

~

"Take the wagon on back to Indabas, friend Bawaith, and deliver the money I collected to Vasale." He trusted the man to do this. "I do not think you will see me again."

"You choose to walk a dangerous road, friend Saj. I wish you good fortune." The driver urged his oxen forward. Saj looked up the slope toward the cave of the priests of Munu and then began climbing.

The little priest named Xit was waiting at the entrance. "Kambak did not expect you quite so soon, but I saw your approach." Was he watching the road or did he have the second sight? It was immaterial. Saj followed him into the cavern.

The High Priest expressed surprise on seeing him. Apparently Xit had not seen necessary to keep him informed. "Welcome again to our humble shrine, Master Saj." He gave him a smug and knowing look. "You are ready perhaps to deal with us now?"

"That depends on what you can offer me, your holiness."

Kambak smiled at the honorific. He undoubtedly knew Saj was attempting to flatter him but probably liked being so addressed anyway. "The statue is still yours. But we can also offer you the woman you — love? Do you think our Saj loves her, Xit?"

"Not yet. But he will."

Saj realized that this was almost certainly true. "I do doubt that she loves me," he said. Whether that, too, would come, he had no idea. Xit offered no words on this subject. "But I feel obligated to rescue her, none the less." From what? A bad marriage? That was hardly his concern, yet — it was his path. He did not doubt it.

"And we can assist you in this," spoke the High Priest. "We shall help you get the Lady — what's her name?"

"Marana," offered his second.

"Yes, Lady Marana. We can get her beyond her father's walls and then conceal her here until you, um, complete your promised task."

"Would not the thegn be able to track her here? His dogs would surely catch her scent." Saj thought of those slavering, toothy jaws with some trepidation.

"This can be hidden," said Xit. "As you and she can be hidden."

Kambak nodded. "The rest of us are naught more than ordinary priests, but our Xit here is a minor sorcerer. I believe he can do as he says."

Xit said nothing, but stood smiling at Saj.

"Very well. If we can get Marana safely away from Sarowhem, then I give my word to track down your stones. But if I fail or perish, you must promise to take care of her and help her go wherever she may wish."

"That seems reasonable," spoke the High Priest. "It is agreed."

"And now we must kidnap a Sharshite noblewoman," said Saj.

"I think," Xit told him, "that she may actually be kidnapping you."

~

It was dark. Well, of course it was — it was night. It wouldn't do to try to break in during the day. A thin crescent sat in the sky, a clear sky of stars.

"You need to see where the lady is being kept," spoke Xit. "That sort of thing is your gift. Then I can get us there."

"Won't the dogs catch our scent?" Saj knew there were guard dogs here, even if Hurrum's hounds were closed in their kennel.

"That is not a matter for magic," his companion told him. "Not that I could not use it but I would rather not spend myself on such spells tonight. Rub some of this on yourself." He handed him a small stone jar of some sort of balm. "It will mask our odor. Plenty, now."

Xit had traded his saffron robe for a kilt, and wore nothing more. His lean body glistened from the ointment he had rubbed into his skin.

The pair crept forward "There are some very ancient wardings here," Xit said. "Interesting. I wish I had time to study them. Nothing I can not handle, though."

Saj had been attempting to figure out where Lady Marana might be. He did know where the family's private rooms lay, but there was no guarantee that the wayward noblewoman had been allowed to return to her own suite. Saj attempted to picture her in his mind.

In the stables? No. Why had that come to him? Oh, yes, that should be the way they leave. Well, try to use logic then. Wherever she might be sleeping, there would be guards without her door. They need only look for them.

Getting past those guards would be another matter. As they moved forward, doors were found to be unlatched, hanging open. That was Xit's work, Saj knew. They were in the family wing of the villa now, in a hallway near the thegn's own rooms. "There, I would wager," whispered Saj, as the pair peeped around a corner to spy a sleepy sentry outside a door, an oil lamp flickering beside him.

Xit nodded. "The door I can force by magic. The guard — you must attend to him, my young friend."

"You can't put him to sleep or something?" grumbled Saj.

"You might try singing a lullaby to him," came the answer. "I can conceal your approach, to some degree. Not make you invisible, you understand, but pull some shadow around you."

Better than nothing, thought Saj. He crept toward the sentry, short sword in hand — and in scabbard. Saj had never slain a man and did not wish to change that now. At the last moment, the guard realized someone was standing near to him. Too late! Saj swung the sword, hilt first, into the man's skull. Down he went.

The young Mur hoped it had not been a fatal strike but had no time to find out. The door swung open before him.

"It is about time," said the Lady Marana.

Beyond her lay her mother, fast asleep on a feather bed. This must be Lady Belema's chamber. Marana raised a finger to her lips, grabbed a small bag, and stepped out into the hall, only glancing at the downed sentry. Already packed to go? She has more faith in me than I have in myself, Saj told himself. And Saj had considerable faith in himself.

Once a dog yapped, as they made their way toward the stables. Neither of his companions asked Saj why he chose this route; for that matter, Saj wasn't quite sure himself. "Are we going to steal horses?" whispered Marana. No, that wouldn't do. There would be too much noise involved.

He looked about once they were inside, still unsure. Rows of stalls lined the room; a horse whinnied softly. "Where does that lead?" he asked, pointing to a large double door at the far end of the barn.

"To the boat house," came the answer.

~

"I would not recommend returning to the cave. There is no reason to give the priests a hostage."

Saj was surprised by Xit's advice. "Are you betraying your own order?" he asked.

"I only served them for a time. I am not one of them."

"But I have promised to gather the stones, the Eyes, for them. I would not back out of a contract."

"Nor should you." They paddled onward for a while in silence, intending to get as far up the Chas before sunrise as possible. Saj suspected that the thegn would think they went the opposite direction, if one small missing boat happened to be noticed at all.

"Where did those shadows come from?" asked Saj, after a time. "The ones you gathered around me last night."

"I pulled them here from other worlds. That is pretty much how all magic works."

"You are a wizard?" Marana asked. She had been sitting in the middle of the boat, peering out into the dark, first to one side, then the other. All this was no doubt a great adventure to her and not particularly dangerous. At worst, she would be taken home again to marry a man she disliked. Xit and Saj would assuredly not fare so well.

"Is that how my, um, dreams work?" Saj had never understood how they came to him.

"In a way. That is not a conversation for here and now."

True, Saj told himself. The faintest light of dawn was beginning to reveal the broad River Chas to them. It was indeed a mighty river here, by far the largest the young man had ever seen. There was little sign of habitation along it, yet enough that they would soon need to pull to the shore and hide for the day.

"Let's stop here," he said, and turned their punt toward the willow-lined southern bank.

SETTING II.
THE EARTH STONE

6.

"You dreamed, did you not?"

"I did, Xit, I dreamed of the Eyes. Again. Though I did not know what they were the last time."

"Do you know where they lie?"

Saj stood and pointed out each direction. "North. East. South. West." He smiled wryly. "Beyond that, I can not say. But I do know that one is not that far away. The golden one. Amber?"

"Topaz," replied the wizard. "All four gems were in fact carved from a single stone. It is near you say?"

"Yes, to the south."

"Oh. Of course. It is the Earth Stone and south is the direction of the earth element."

"I saw a man with a crown. The stone was in that crown."

"That must be the Pretender," chimed in Marana. "His court is to the south."

Saj and Xit turned toward her. "What are we to do with her?" asked the Mur.

"Don't ask him, boy! Ask me what I intend to do," came Marana's peeved response.

"And what do you intend, my lady?" asked Xit.

"Why to go with you on your quest." She eyed Saj. "There had to be a reason you rescued me. It was so I could help you!"

Saj shrugged. "Maybe so, my lady." Xit looked doubtful.

"It is her choice," continued the young man. "After all, there must have been *some* reason we rescued the Lady Marana." He turned to the noblewoman. "Just exactly what did we rescue you from, if I might ask?"

"A forced marriage to Lord Gawif. The man is twice my age and has so many mistresses he needed to add a wing to his villa!"

"I have heard of him," spoke Xit. "As to the womanizing, I can not speak, but he is also known as a hard and cruel man. An ambitious man who would tie your family to those ambitions."

Saj considered this information. "Well, no lass should marry where she does not wish. We do not do things so in Muradon."

"I've known Muram women," Xit said. "They would be likely to knife a man if forced to marry him."

"Very true," agreed Saj. "I guess we can't have you knifing Lord Gawif, my lady."

"I might enjoy it," she muttered.

~

Northward they paddled that night, further up River Chas. Yes, it was the opposite direction from where the Earth Stone lay but Marana, who seemed to have a good grasp on the region's geography, told them a tributary stream could lead them to the Pretender's very door.

"He is a grand-nephew — I think — of the last true Sharshite king," she informed them. "So he claims the crown now, but hides away in a remote keep and does little but collect tribute from those who still follow him." Her disdain was not hidden. "My father and his father before him recognized that the Mura are here to stay and have brought order to our land."

"And prosperity," added Saj. "Without healthy trade, no nation can endure."

Days passed, through which they still hid from any eyes. Nights passed, spent paddling, until they reached their turning. It was a sizable river too, and flowed directly from the south, at least at first.

What Marana had not known, having seen only maps, was that the river would become impassable rapids and falls after a few days of travel. "We shall have to walk," decided Saj. He considered himself the leader of this group and neither of the others had objected, so far.

"We shall need to find food, too," Marana reminded him. They were not equipped for hunting — aside from the sling Saj still carried — and what provisions they had brought were running out. Money they had; both the girl and the wizard had made certain to bring along a quantity of coins and even Saj was not without a few to jingle in his purse. Alas, there was no place to spend them.

"Can't you bring us some steaks from another world?" he asked Xit.

"I could, but bringing something that solid requires a considerable effort. Moreover, they would disappear from your stomach after a while, drawn back to where they belong."

"At least berries are in season," said Lady Marana.

On they trudged, the land gradually rising. Maybe I'll see those mountains after all, thought Saj. It was definitely an empty land; what few folk there were hid from them as they approached. Here on the borders between Muram Sharsh and the lands that did not acknowledge that rule, there were constant skirmishes and unrest, and the inhabitants knew to avoid outsiders of any sort.

They themselves hid when bodies of armed men approached. Who was to know whom they might serve and how they might treat wanderers such as themselves? If they were noticed by those passing troops, it was probably assumed that they were simply peasants scuttling from their path.

~

"We turn here," Saj announced one morning. Neither of his companions thought to question this. "We draw near to the stone," he later whispered to Xit.

"Do we simply walk into this Pretender's court?" wondered the sorcerer.

"I do not think we would be able to sneak in," Saj replied. "It might be best to be bold."

"You with your Muram looks might not find welcome."

"You stand out a bit yourself, Xit."

"I think," said Xit, "that it might be wise to let the lady take the lead on this and we act the role of servitors." He had spoken this loud enough that Marana could hear it.

"You should keep in mind," she told them, "that they speak only Sharshic in the court. No Muram from you two!"

Xit answered her in what sounded to Saj to be perfect Sharshic, even down to the accent. He had best take some lessons from his companions.

"However," continued Marana, "the idea of a Sharshite noble-woman traveling the wilds with a pair like you is rather preposterous. Better we pose as merchants." She eyed Saj. "I shall play wife and interpreter."

"Ah, returning to Lorj after trading successfully in the north," Xit said. "That might work."

"But an odd route to be taking," admitted Marana.

"Oh, we are avoiding the pirates," spoke Saj. "Haven't you heard that they are particularly numerous this year? I can even provide tales of how we escaped them."

Following Saj's new direction, they soon enough reached a decent road, obviously used at least on occasion. Following that road through rugged hill country, they reached a village and then another.

~

"I do not like it," proclaimed Xit, staring at Lady Marana. She had chosen to crop her hair short, dispensing with her braids.

Saj was not so certain. He sipped some more of the ale in his tankard. The young Mur was not much of a drinker and had never cared for ale, but that apparently was all they served in this inn. "It is practical, I will admit," he ventured at last. "And it might make you less recognizable if anyone happens to be looking for you."

"That was my thought, Husband." Marana had insisted that they refer to each other so, practicing their roles before reaching the court of Flawum, the self-styled Ri of Sharsh, the Pretender.

Saj thought perhaps he would like Marana to play wife in earnest. But that was not an idea to dwell on right now.

"It might help even more if you could dye it or cover it with a wig, Wife."

Xit shook his head. "Not much chance of finding either dyes or wigs here." He smiled, and added, "Mistress Bela," that being her chosen alias. There seemed no reason for Xit to assume a false name, but Saj now went by Tomik, a similarly common name in Muradon and usually shortened to simply 'Tom.'

They were, at last, clean, rested, fed. They were also practically in the shadow of the Pretender's castle. Tomorrow, they should present themselves.

7.

"We are travelers, asking safe passage through your kingdom, your highness."

Flawum looked upon the young Sharshite woman with mild interest. He shifted a gout-swollen foot upon its pillow, grimaced, and spoke. "Few merchants choose to pass this way," he observed, "and none as comely as you."

Saj wonders what we are saying to each other, thought Marana. *He looks unhappy.* "I thank you, my lord," she demurely replied. "We seek only to return to Matanas, having lost much of our trade goods to pirates."

"Ah, yes, I have heard they are bold this year. We must deal with them." He turned a suspicious eye to Saj. "Your husband is Muram."

"Yes, highness. He is a good man, if a bit simple. I have always run the business."

She knew Xit must be smirking behind her back. "The other is our slave, a man from the Southern Isles."

"Slavery is not permitted here. What is your name, man?" he asked.

"Xit, oh great lord," the little man replied, bowing deeply.

"Well, know that slavery is a Muram institution. If you wish to remain here, you are a free man."

That is rather admirable, thought Marana. *Perhaps I have misjudged this would-be king. And I definitely should not have laid it on so thick, claiming Xit was a slave.*

"Oh, thank you, your royal highness," breathed Xit. "Ha!" he said to Marana. She could scarcely keep herself from breaking into laughter. *Yet — Flawum thinking Xit a grateful freed slave could give them an advantage here. It would put some space between them and allow the wizard to act more freely.*

"As you will, my lord," she quietly said. "Xit has served well and I willingly release him."

"Excellent, excellent. I say, my girl, you should dine with me tonight. Your husband too, if you must." *Clearly the Pretender would prefer 'Tom' not be there.*

"Thank you, your highness. I am honored." She bowed and backed from his presence. Seven steps, right? She thought she remembered the protocol. Then she turned and left the audience chamber, followed by Xit and Saj.

"Did you see the crown?" she immediately asked the Mur.

"It rested on a pillow on a rock," he said, "over to the left of the throne. Our left."

"That would be the sacred rock on which kings of Sharsh are crowned," she informed him. "I did not know it was here."

"It could be a fake," opined Saj.

"As is this 'king,'" added Xit. "Are you truly going to dine with him?"

"Why not? He can't chase me with that foot of his."

~

"I tried to converse with him of cavalry strategies but Flawum was quite uninterested. He will never attempt to take on the Mura, of that I am sure. So I gave him a convoluted cock-and-bull story as to my aristocratic origins and how I met my beloved Tomik in Matanas."

"He didn't make any, um, advances, did he?" asked Saj.

"And what concern would that be of yours?" she snapped. At the young man's crestfallen look, she added, "No, no, he only flirted some. I think our Pretender knows his limits. So," Marana asked, "what were you two up to?"

Saj held a bit of thick amber-colored glass. "If I can slip this into the setting on the crown, perhaps no one will be the wiser. At least for a while." He held it up and looked through it. "It was part of a window until I put a rock through it."

"It wouldn't fool anyone close up," said Xit.

"It might not need to," he replied.

"There do not seem to be any magics around the crown, other than the Eye itself," reported Xit. "No protection nor alarms. The throne room is not well guarded, either. I was able to slip in for a few moments and no one noticed."

"I wish I could see something about this," sighed Saj.

"It is near impossible to see ones own actions," Xit said. "But you know that."

"How does Saj see things?" asked Marana. "You said you would explain."

Xit composed himself for a few seconds. "The gift of Saj is not unlike my own. It is only expressed a little differently. Where I, shall we say, reach into other worlds, he is seeing into them.

"The thing is, there are an infinite number of worlds, of universes, out there. A seer can sort through them, after a fashion, and find things that are to come. In Saj's case — indeed, in most cases — this is quite unconscious. Prophetic dreams and such. There are few seers who can truly harness their gift."

Saj broke in. "Infinite worlds?"

"One differing in the tiniest of details from the next but, spread across infinity, all things can exist." He paused. "All things do and *must* exist. That seems overwhelming to most of us, but there are some —" He looked toward Saj. "Who are capable of finding their way through it, seeing a chain of events threading through an ultimately random and infinite multiverse.

"It might be said that each action, no matter how infinitesimal, leads to another universe. Whether that universe was created then or always existed, not even the gods can say."

"If I were to decide to turn right rather than left, would that create a new universe?" came Marana's question.

"Not exactly, for you can and will turn only one direction at that moment. It is inevitable — cause and effect rule at this level, and that is why the future can be seen. But the basic fabric of Being is random in its actions; from that stems the infinite worlds that can — and may or may not — exist. Nor does it actually matter whether they do or don't."

"I shall always turn the same way? Then I have no free will?"

"Of course you do. A choice is made, and no one and nothing forces it."

"You two are hurting my head," complained Saj. "I'd just as soon not know how it works."

"You still don't, really," Xit said. He rose. "Now that I am a free man, I have been offered my own room — no more sleeping on my owners' floor! So I will leave the married couple here and go find a good night's rest."

~

"I know that man," hissed Marana. Saj turned to see a burly red-headed soldier alighting from his horse. "He is a retainer of Gawif," she told him. She puzzled for a moment, trying to think of something, then shook her head. "I can not recall his name. But he is not a good man."

"Gawif? Then he has dealings with this Pretender." Saj smiled. "I imagine the Viceroy would enjoy hearing of that."

"I am more concerned with what current business brings him to Flawum's court."

"Perhaps you. Perhaps not. They would not expect us to come here."

"Even so, we might become a subject of gossip. It wouldn't take Flawum long to put things together."

"Then we must act soon." Saj watched the visitor disappear into the Pretender's relatively modest and somewhat run-down fortress. "Would this man recognize you?"

"I think not. I have watched many men from windows who never saw me in return." She smiled a bit at the memories. Her life will never be like that again, thought Saj.

"We could forget that jewel and just head to Lorj, you know," she said softly.

"I did make a bargain," he replied. "But more importantly, I think I am meant to gather these Eyes of the Wind."

"A quest." She nodded. "Then you must complete it." Marana paused, considering what she had just said. "*We* must complete it."

There was little to do there other than rest and pretend to await the permission of Ri Flawum to travel across his supposed realm. At least they were well fed as the Pretender's guests.

Xit joined the pair toward evening. "There is gossip in the

court," reported the sorcerer. "It is said that the Tiarna Gawif — yes, they give him one of the old, outlawed titles of nobility — is searching for his runaway fiance. Stolen by a Muram fellow, some think. Others believe she jumped into the river and drowned herself." He chuckled softly. "Some say they would do the same if betrothed to Gawif."

"It crossed my mind," admitted Marana. "Though I thought it would be better to shove him in."

"We need to act," Saj stated. "We need to act tonight."

8.

"We will need horses."

"I've had my eye on some," Marana reported. "I shall have them ready and waiting." There was no denying that the noblewoman was the best suited for anything to do with horses.

"I have watched. No one enters the throne room after our Pretender goes to his dinner. Those who clean, do so in the morning, for Flawum sleeps late and never holds court till near noon. There is a sentry outside at all hours," Xit went on, "but I think we can get around him one way or another. You won't need to bash his head in, my boy."

"It would be noticed," Saj responded seriously. He was in no mood for banter right now.

"That it would. The earlier we can accomplish this, the better, for it will give us more of the night for our escape. No one is likely to note that we are gone until morning." He shrugged. "And who knows when anyone might notice the Earth Stone had been replaced?"

"You could have had a career as a burglar, Master Xit," spoke Marana.

With a smile, he replied, "Who ever said I didn't?"

It was at that moment a servant in livery of Flawum's colors — red and gold, and rather shabby — appeared at their chamber's door. "Mistress Bela," said he, "his Royal Highness requests your attendance at dinner." Did the man leer just a little in the direction of Marana? Saj clenched a fist and then released it. Not worth it, not worth it, he told himself.

"I shall try to be ready," she told her companions, as she wrapped a silk shawl, a gift from the Pretender delivered earlier that day, about her shoulders. She followed the attendant down the hall toward the private suite of Flawum.

"I fear our host does not have good intentions," slowly spoke Xit.

"I know he doesn't," Saj replied. "We must trust our Bela to take care of herself."

~

"I shall remain outside while you do the job," whispered Xit. "My task is to distract our guardsman. And perhaps I can throw a little shadow on you to help you get through the door unnoted."

"It will be unlocked?" asked Saj.

"I've already taken care of that. It is among the easiest of spells. I think even you could master it, as you do have some talent."

"Thank you but no, my friend! I am happy to remain ignorant of all your magic."

A minute later, the dark, diminutive wizard was bending the sentry's ear with some story or another. Saj slipped into the throne room without problem.

He felt the piece of glass in his pouch. Saj had carefully ground and polished it into a form that resembled the precious stone he intended to steal. There it was, as before. He reached out and put his hand upon the Earth Stone.

Saj fell back, stunned. Such power! Could he even hold that gem? Gingerly, he reached forward again, placed a fingertip on its facets. It tingled, but it wasn't so bad now. But he was seeing things, things he knew were not there, things he had only seen before in dream. Block them out and get to the work at hand!

Carefully, with a small metal rod Xit had given him, he pried the stone from its setting. For a moment, he held it in his hand, staring into its depths. No, don't, he told himself. He slipped it into his pouch and pressed the colored glass into the space where the Eye had once shone. The glass did not really shine; he could readily see the difference. To a casual, distant viewer, one who suspected nothing, it would not be so.

He bent the retainers to grasp this new gem, a gem suited to a Pretender, in its place in the Crown of Sharsh. Done. Saj rose and returned to the door, opening it only a crack. Another man had joined the sentry and Xit, and the three stood gossiping. Worse, the newcomer faced directly toward the door. He would surely be seen if he opened any wider.

Nothing to do but wait. His hand went to the gem in his pouch. It felt warm and he felt a great urge to pull it out, to again peer into it. Neither Xit nor the priests of Munu had given him any warning of this. Had they not known?

Again he peeked. Ah, the third man had departed and the sentry's back was to him. Hoping Xit's shadows were still in place, Saj slipped out and up the hall a short way. Then he turned and walked back openly, so the guard would see him approach. "Hail, friend Xit," he said and passed by.

The Baxac wizard would follow shortly, as planned.

~

"How long should we wait?" wondered Saj.

"I know no better than you," answered Xit.

There had been no Marana at their rendezvous. Half an hour later, there had still been no Marana. Saj continued to sense the stone in his pouch.

At last he said, "Perhaps you should keep this," and offered the entire bag to the sorcerer. He feared to pull out the stone.

Xit backed away. "Not I, Saj! It may call to you but it might well destroy me." Then Xit had known of its dangers. "We must give the stones to Marana for safekeeping as we gather them."

Saj nodded and tucked the pouch away. "She had best come soon."

"She could only be with the Pretender," said Xit. "You felt she could handle him and I think you were right."

"None the less, I believe I shall go scouting for her. You remain here and I shall return shortly." Saj left the wizard there, in a secluded corner of the courtyard before Flawum's gates, and slipped back into the keep. People came and went at all hours and he was known by now, needing do no more than give a friendly nod to the sentries. I don't even need Xit's shadows here, he thought, as he crept down the dark and empty hallways.

A lone sentry dozed before the entrance to the Pretender's suite. Saj had not been there before but Marana had given him a good

47

description of the way. He was upon the man and still he went unnoticed. No, the sentry's head snapped up, eyes wide. Hardly thinking of his actions, Saj thrust his hand to the man's chin and shoved the back of his head into the stone wall behind him. The guard slumped and slid to the floor.

Twice now I've bashed some poor fellow's head, he told himself. This is no work for an honest merchant. He eased the door open. There was the dinner table, in a room where a few candles still flickered. Many must have burned earlier but they were spent stumps now.

A noise from an adjoining chamber. And light. Saj investigated, carefully.

There was Marana. And what was she wearing? Armor? Yes, of sorts, mostly leather but still — well, serviceable. And oddly attractive on her. On the bed lay the Pretender, more-or-less still in his clothes, tied up and gagged with an assortment of multicolored silk kerchiefs.

Marana turned to the door and smiled broadly. "He wanted to make love to a warrior maiden. So I told him I must first make him my captive, and tied him up."

"Mmmffff!" said Flawum.

"I'm sorry about this, your highness. I think you're not such a bad fellow, really, but he is my husband, you know, and we really must get to Matanas."

Saj nearly laughed aloud at these fabrications. The Pretender would know them as such soon, realize that Mistress Bela was in truth the Lady Marana of Sarowhem. But muddying the water now might gain them a day or two.

Marana threw her shawl around herself. "Let's get out of here," she said. "The sooner the better."

9.

Leaving the keep had proven no more difficult than entering. Xit gave the Lady Marana's armored form a good looking-over when they reached him, but said nothing of it. "Can we still get the horses?" he asked.

"Follow me. You have the stone?"

"We do. And —" Xit looked at Saj before continuing. "We think it might be best if you carried it. The Eye, um, does things to us."

"Can it hurt you?"

"Maybe," said Saj. "It certainly is distracting and we need all our attention right now."

"It should not affect you at all," added Xit.

"Very well." She held out a gauntleted hand. Marana looked over the gem Saj placed in her palm, shrugged, and slipped it into a poke. "The mounts I had my eye on are kept over here." They followed her between a couple shabby outhouses to a small corral, containing four horses.

"I've taken some time to make friends with them," she announced, as they came to the fence and nuzzled at her. Saj was no judge of horses but these looked good enough. "There are saddles in that shack over there." Marana nodded toward an open shed beside the corral. "Get with it."

She can be pretty bossy, thought Saj. Her upbringing, I suppose. But he hurried to do her bidding. Saddles, bridles — they were worn, some of the leather even seemed a bit moldy, but they could not be choosy at this moment. Ropes. They could lead the fourth horse.

Marana steadied the horses as the two men fumbled with saddling them. That neither was skilled at this was obvious. "Tighten that more," she ordered Xit, when she looked over their work. "Good enough," was her assessment, otherwise. "Let's ride."

Xit gave her a bow. "Thank you for your patience, my lady. I am sure it was hard for you to hold your tongue." Marana had to smile at that; it must have been all too true.

"Which way do we ride?" the little sorcerer asked. The question was directed at Saj.

"East. Toward the Fire Stone."

"But maybe south first," recommended Marana, "in case anyone sees us. It should look like we are trying to get to the southern coast."

~

They had still managed to slip from the Pretender's compound before midnight. That was not so bad. No more than half a mile south did they go, before cutting eastward, away from the road they traveled. It seemed a well-used road, dirt but maintained and graded from time to time. Some commerce must travel up it from the south. Smugglers, they would have to be, as the Mura controlled the coasts down there, the mainland coasts that lay north of Lorj.

This made sense to Saj. Being a center for smuggling would help finance the Pretender's court, allow him to maintain some power here. It might be useful to know that if he ever got to Lorj.

No, when he got to Lorj. He would reach that southern island and make his own fortune there. But would this self-possessed young noblewoman still be at his side?

Now they rode through untracked wilderness, in a generally eastward direction. There were impenetrable thickets, here and there among the tall forest trees, that they must skirt. "If we come upon any sort of path it would probably be safe to follow it now," felt Xit. He turned his head toward Saj. "So where is the next Eye? The Fire Stone, I would wager."

Saj nodded toward the northeast. "Somewhere up there. I think it is in the mountains."

In mid-afternoon they struck a narrow path leading more-or-less in their intended direction. "We could have been paralleling this all day," mused Saj.

Xit nodded. "Just as well we stayed off any traveled way until now."

"What if we meet anyone?" Marana asked. "What is our plan?"

Of course, there was no plan. Saj had not really thought ahead. "You should change out of that, um, outfit," he told her. "It makes you rather memorable."

STEPHEN BROOKE

"At least pull a cloak around yourself if we come on anyone," added Xit.

"Do you think I could pass for a man?" she asked them.

Well, she is tall and broad of shoulder, thought Saj. He and the noblewoman were of the same height, in fact. But she had definite feminine curves to her and a full womanly bosom. "I wouldn't chance it," he replied.

They camped beneath the great oaks of the forest that night, not risking a fire.

"Poor Flawum would have been discovered hours ago," said Marana. "I wonder if he has realized who we are yet."

Saj answered. "Someone will eventually. Then Gawif, and everyone else who is interested, will know where you were."

"But not where I am."

"None would expect us to travel this direction," agreed the Mur.

"Ah, but according to our Xit it is the only direction we could have traveled." Marana laughed. It was the first time Saj had heard her do so and he hoped it was not the last.

"Then," spoke the wizard, "let us hope that everyone else was meant to turn the other direction."

~

Hoof beats behind them. The sound was unmistakable. "One horse," said Marana, "and traveling quickly."

"Can we run?" asked Saj.

"These are decent enough mounts," she replied, "but they would win no races."

There was no point in going further. They sat in their saddles and waited. As they waited, Saj unobtrusively slipped his sling from the pouch at his waist.

"It is Gawif's man," came Marana's level voice, as their pursuer came into view, a powerful warhorse beneath him. The man's red hair — he wore no helmet nor cap — and burly form were readily recognizable.

He was a mounted soldier, a man skilled with lance and sword.

51

No one of them could stand against him with these weapons, nor even all three together. The man reined in his steed and sat regarding the group.

"So, Lady Marana, are you ready to return to your intended husband? It was not so hard to guess that you would not go south." He scornfully looked upon Xit and Saj. "These two are not worth the bother of slaying. Come with me and I shall let them go."

"Don't believe him," whispered Xit.

"I don't," came Marana's low reply.

Saj had slid from the saddle. He would need both feet firmly planted. The young man stepped away from the horses and whirled his sling over his head.

The first hurled stone struck the soldier squarely in his chest, a chest protected solely by a thick leather vest. The man grunted, and reeled in his saddle, but was not badly wounded. He roared in anger and charged forward, sword in hand.

By then, Saj had another stone in the pouch of his sling. This one took their attacker in the forehead. He fell from his horse and did not again move.

So he truly had slain a man this time. Most likely. Saj did not intend to check.

But Marana did. "We could use his horse and equipment," she spoke. "No sense in wasting them." It took some time for her and Xit to get the steed calmed and under control.

Saj stood gazing toward the form on the ground. There was a pool of blood beneath the man's head. Finally, Xit went to examine the body.

"He is still breathing. We should slip a knife into him." He looked from Saj to Marana. "Neither of you has the stomach for that sort of thing, do you?" He again lowered his eyes to the wounded man. "Nor do I," he admitted.

"But I am more than willing to strip him of his weapons and armor," stated Marana, "and leave his survival in the hands of the gods."

Saj shook his head. "That might be more cruel than dispatching him."

"The gods are often cruel, friend Saj," spoke Xit.

~

Marana now rode their assailant's former horse. It was a far better mount than the other four, tall and more than a bit bad-tempered. That did not seem to bother the noblewoman, but she warned the others to give the stallion a wide berth.

"I shall name you Ri," she told the horse. It offered no objections. As they rode through the rest of the day, she would from time to time cast covert glances at Saj. He had been heroic, hadn't he? So calm and businesslike about defending them!

Yet only a very uncertain young man in the aftermath. Marana thought she liked that. Saj was human. Saj was real, not a figure from one of the romances she had read.

Eastward they continued. It was likely that there would be no more pursuit from the Pretender's hold. Flawum might have been humiliated but there was no reason to send men after them and no profit in doing so. Even if he had any idea of where they were.

Until someone eventually discovered the Eye had been stolen. That would change things. He would most certainly send word to Gawif of their visit and that word would also reach the Thegn Hurrum. There would be those who would be keeping an eye out for the travelers.

Saj rode mostly in silence that day. At last he spoke, perhaps to no one but himself. "Was this something I was destined to do?"

"No more than anything else," answered Xit. "You did what was needed at the moment."

"You would not change it, would you?" asked Marana.

"I do not know. I do not know if it could have been changed."

Xit shrugged. "There may be things that can't be changed, but we shall never know that unless we keep trying to change them."

"I would change nothing we have so far done," Marana firmly stated. All in all, she felt that her adventure was playing out nicely.

"Very well," replied Saj. "I guess we had best get busy changing what is to come."

Setting III.
THE FIRE STONE

10.

Mountains. Saj gazed upon their heights at last. There were mountains on the Muram peninsula but nothing like these. The trio had been rising toward those mountains, their way ever steeper, the oaks and beeches along their road giving way to tall conifers.

"There is little in this part of Sharsh," said Marana. She did not say it very loudly for there was something about this land that led one to use hushed tones. One felt very small here.

"If this can even be considered Sharsh," remarked Xit. "Do you know yet where we go, boy?" he asked of Saj.

"I have seen — fire. That makes sense, right? It is the Fire Stone." He paused a moment to gather himself. "A mountain of fire. There are such, I have heard."

"A volcano. Ah. There are some in the southern mountains. Most are long dormant." He gave his young friend a smile. "If you seek active ones, this Lorj of which you constantly speak has more of those."

"No," Saj replied, ignoring the jest in his comrade's voice, "it is there." He pointed almost due east.

"Isn't that where the Sorceress of the Mountains dwells?" whispered Marana.

"Probably," came Xit's cheerful answer.

"I do not know who that is," spoke Saj. "I only feel the Eye somewhere near, glowing with its own red fires." He sighed deeply. "Let's break camp and go find it."

Two more days they climbed, higher into the range. There was a good enough road that seemed to lead in the proper direction. Those were peaceful days, days when their quest could be put out of Saj's mind. He would rather think of Marana. Did she really have any interest in him other than as a way to escape Gawif? Her suggestion of heading for Lorj seemed to suggest that she wished to stay with him.

Suddenly, across the still late afternoon air, a word rang out, a command, but in no language Saj knew. None the less, he and his companions reined in their mounts, assuming they were being told to halt.

A man stepped forth in light armor of the old Sharshite infantry pattern, much of it leather but with metal bands around the torso and a conical helmet. He held a short, heavy spear; the short sword that hung at his waist was practically identical to Saj's own. Again, the language he spoke was unintelligible to Saj. To Marana, too, it seemed, but Xit answered in the same tongue.

The two conversed for quite a while, with the soldier taking an occasional appraising look at Marana and Saj. Just what was that little wizard telling him? Their entire story? After a bit, the man gave them a little bow, stepped aside, and waved them up the road. "You should know," said Xit, as they proceeded, "that many arrows were aimed at us from the forest."

"So I assumed," replied Marana. Saj hadn't really been thinking of such things but, of course, the man would not have been guarding the road all alone.

"What was that language?" he asked.

"Ildin. You will hear much of it where we go. Indeed," Xit went on, "if you ever make it to Lorj, you will find it common there, too."

"I've heard of the Ildin people," remarked Marana. "There were many of them once, weren't there?"

"There still are. Just not around these parts."

Saj recalled that the statue in the cave of the priests depicted some Ildin god. Banat? Was that it?

They saw no more soldiers, nor anyone else, before nightfall.

~

At dawn, however, they saw many soldiers. Their leader addressed them in Muram.

"The Cana has charged us to accompany you to her court," said he.

Xit smiled very broadly. "The Cana. That is a title I have not heard in — well, you would not believe how long it has been."

"I do not know the name," Saj replied to this.

"The Cana is both our holy mountain and our queen," the captain of their escort informed him.

"'Cana' means something like 'consecrated' in the ancient tongue of Tesra," Xit whispered to his comrades later, as they made their way up the road, soldiers both before and behind them. To keep with the pace of their escort, they walked, leading the horses. At places, it grew steep and would have been a difficult ride anyway, more stairs than road.

"That must be their holy mountain," said Xit, as a snow-topped cone came into sight. "It does not seem to be letting off steam right now."

"It makes me nervous," admitted Saj. He glanced at Marana but she seemed quite calm and quite interested in what was going on. They were in a long valley; grass and wild flowers grew about them and sheep grazed here and there. Houses could be spied in the distances, closer to the slopes on either side.

Well ahead could be seen a larger edifice, not a keep nor even a manor house, but standing high. "That, I would guess, is the residence of the Cana," Xit said.

"It is," the captain told him. "Our lady awaits you."

It was a house of wood, with a tall peaked roof. Indeed, most of the house seemed to be roof, with low buttressed walls below it. "I think everyone here lives in the attic," quipped Marana. "It's an odd sort of house, isn't it?"

"Snow would slide off such a roof," Saj told her. "They must get a lot of it here."

"Oh. We have very little where I live." She frowned. "Where I used to live."

"There's none at all in Lorj," he said. Let her make of that what she would.

THE EYES OF THE WIND

They did not enter that house immediately, for the Cana, the ruler of these people, stood before it on a high porch, wrapped in a red robe.

Those people, Saj noted, were generally of modest height and darker than the typical Sharshite. As dark as my own people, thought he, though with a skin tone more olive than bronze. To his eyes, they looked rather like Paxo whom he met in Indabas.

The language they spoke to one another he did not understand, but assumed it was the Ildin tongue.

Their queen also seemed dark, darker than those she ruled. The woman stood looking down on them, her gaze going from one face to the next until it rested on Xit's. She looked sharply at the small dark man; with recognition came a smile.

"I know you, Crocodile."

"My greetings, Mec Lura."

She laughed at this. "And to you. How should I name you?"

"Xit will do, my lady."

Her eyes returned to Marana and Saj. "I may know you but your friends, I see, do not."

"For now, Mec."

She nodded and spoke to them. "You two are welcome in our valley. Your Xit and I are old friends." She glanced in the sorcerer's direction. "You might not believe how old. Enter my house, and I shall give you time to rest and clean up and whatever else you wish to do before we speak again." She gave them another look. "Do you share a bed?"

Marana colored up immediately. Perhaps Saj did as well but he gave silent thanks that it did not show so much with his skin tone. "No, my lady," answered the girl.

"Not yet," murmured Saj, only to himself.

"Ah, very well. When you are refreshed, do come and dine in my rooms. You too, of course, Crocodile."

11.

"Lura is her name," Xit told them. "It is from the Old Speech, the language of Tesra. That is a tongue that goes back immeasurable ages, ages forgotten by man. The name might be translated as 'starlight.'"

"You called her something else," said Saj.

"Yes, 'Mec.' It is a title, also from that language, meaning something like 'lady' or even 'queen.' I suspect it has been many years since she has heard either." He reconsidered that. "Perhaps centuries. Yes, Lura may appear of middle-age but she is much, much older."

"I had read that Tesrans were long lived," said Marana. "I — I didn't really believe. There is so much nonsense written down in books."

"This you may believe. She is of the race of Tesra, come here across the Great Sea into exile, after the Mura sacked her city." He shook his head. "The place was already much fallen and many had abandoned it."

"The Old Tongue. That is the language also know as Zikem, isn't it?" Saj asked in a subdued voice.

Xit was more than simply surprised. "I have not heard it called that in — um, I shouldn't really say how long. How do you know of that, lad?"

"Remember that it was my race that conquered Tesra. Books from there have found their way across the sea." He shrugged. "I am no scholar, friend Xit, but I have listened to those who are." He looked about the little wood-paneled room in which they had been installed. Three narrow beds were fitted into the space, but one he suspected had been added only now. One wall sloped inward toward the ceiling, indicating that it was part of the roof. "When will we be called to dinner?"

"I think she may simply expect us to show up," offered Marana.

"And I think you are probably right," Xit said. "At worst, we shall end up sitting and talking with her until food appears."

"We'll have to ask directions," said Saj, as the three exited into a narrow hallway. "By the way, did you notice the Fire Stone? It was set in her staff or whatever you call it."

"I did," replied Xit. He spoke some words in Ildin to a passing girl. She pointed the way.

"How would we ever get it?" wondered Marana.

"Ask her for it, maybe," said the sorcerer. "She surely knows why we have come."

They were ushered into the Cana's private chambers, surprisingly snug though hardly spartan, and unabashedly feminine. "This is as bad as my mother's rooms," whispered Marana, giving a slightly disapproving look to the pink and red furnishings.

"You should have been a Muram woman," Saj whispered back.

"Maybe I can be persuaded to become one," was the reply. There was no time for Saj to think on all she might mean by that, for their hostess entered at that moment.

~

"These, my people, are Ildin. Their race has mostly been pushed out of their traditional lands, here in the south of what is now Sharsh, or absorbed into the Sharshite populace. Some migrated south into Lorj; more crossed the mountains to dwell in the wide, empty valley that lies there."

The Cana was obviously of a very different people. She was dark of skin, though not quite so much as Xit. Her mass of hair, however, was of a surprising straw color, and somewhat curly. She was unlike anyone Saj had ever encountered and he could not keep himself from staring at her from time to time. He was certain Marana was doing the same.

"You wonder about me," she said, speaking to either or both.

Saj only nodded, but Marana spoke up. "Are you truly as — as old as Xit says?"

"Oh, yes. I maintain my youth by drinking the blood of virgins," she drawled, eyeing Marana in a most disconcerting manner. The girl shrank from that gaze, but Xit chuckled.

"Are you trying to frighten these youngsters, my lady?"

"Perhaps just trying to convince them that virginity is not such a wonderful thing," she replied. "You two are meant for each other, you know."

Marana firmly shook her head. "Not until this quest is completed. Then one may speak to me of marriage."

Lura raised an eyebrow. "I was not necessarily speaking of marriage." She laughed aloud at the girl's expression. "Let me see the Earth Stone, Marana. You are carrying it, aren't you?"

Xit nodded his approval of the request.

"You might as well," said Saj. This woman could take the stone from them should she desire.

Marana took the Eye from some concealed spot in her clothing — Saj could not tell exactly where from his angle — and handed it to the Cana. "Hmm, a bit of a tingle to this one. But different from mine." She handed it back to the Sharshite girl. "Xit thinks I should give you my Fire Stone."

"It is time the Eyes were reunited, Lura."

"Perhaps. As I remember, some trickster god scattered them when I was still young."

"My lady, you are young yet," Xit told her.

"Ah, I do feel young this evening. It is good to have someone new here." She laughed gaily and turned to Xit. "And someone old!

"I think you young people have had enough for this day. Go find your beds — separate, alas — and we shall speak more on this later. But you, Crocodile, remain with me a while."

~

"Why does she call him 'Crocodile?'" wondered Marana. "And are you sure this is the way back to our room?"

"I don't know. And I am. Here we are."

"Do you think they will discuss giving you the Fire Stone?"

"I am certain the lady had other things on her mind. It is unlikely that Xit will return to us tonight."

"Oh." A pause as it sank in. "Oh!" Hadn't she recognized any of that? Marana should have spent more of her life around people and less around horses.

They sat down on those separate beds of theirs, neither in any mood for sleep. "Should I be more like, well, someone like Lura?" asked the girl.

"Be like yourself," Saj replied. "That's always simplest."

"You are good at that. I've always been tugged this way and that to be different people."

"But in the end you chose to be Marana and ran away from what others would force on you. I am glad of that."

"So am I." She rose and came over to sit at the Mur's side. "I said I would not speak of marriage or — or anything else, until we were done with all this. But I wouldn't mind if you held me tonight."

"Neither would I." Saj put his arm around Marana and so it remained for some hours, hours awake, hours of slumber.

They awoke to see Xit standing over them. "When Lura spoke of sharing a bed, I do not think this is what she meant," said the sorcerer. Dawn's light filtered into the room through the tiny window.

Saj sat up. "It's cold in here, isn't it? And we slept without covers all night."

"I had you to keep me warm," Marana answered, and rose. "You two need to get out while I use the chamber pot."

12.

"Our Cana has chosen to give us a task. Or, more precisely, give Saj a task. We," he said to Marana, "shall only assist."

"And then she will give us the Fire Stone?" Saj asked.

"I believe so. Truly, I believe she will give it anyway but we must play her games first."

Later that morning, the Cana called them before her in what amounted to her throne room. The throne on which she sat was no more than a comfortably-upholstered chair and the room itself was somewhat cozy. In her right hand she held her staff, taller than she and with the deep red Fire Stone set in its apex.

"You wish to take my Eye away from me," she spoke, as soon as they were before her. "I shall make this simple and freely give it to you." Lura looked to where Xit stood. "One has convinced me that it should be so.

"First, however, you must complete a task." A smile played briefly on her lips. "What sort of quest would not have a few tests for its heroes?"

The best sort, thought Saj, but he held his tongue.

"I charge you, Saj the Seer — yes, Xit told me you have been so named — to go to the holy mountain, the other Cana, and dream for me. See what you are able and report it."

"That does not seem — too difficult, my lady," said Saj.

"There are some dangers. You must brave the fire spears."

"If I must. When do we leave?" Fire spears? That did not sound good.

"Tomorrow will do. I, ah, need to confer further with Xit this evening."

~

It was a day's journey to the volcano, along a winding dirt road. A rushing stream paralleled that road for much of its distance, before veering off northwards.

"Our little river originates high in the mountains," explained their guide. They had only one, apparently a priestess of some sort,

Ramapee of name. As the Cana, she wore a robe of red. "There is a shrine of sorts at the spring where it first wells up from the rocks."

She looked toward her people's sacred mountain. A faint steamy plume clung to its snow-blanketed summit. "We should arrive before dark," said the priestess and urged her shaggy little pony forward. They did indeed reach a small cottage at the base of the volcano just as dusk settled onto the valley.

"There is a shrine to the god of fire and light, Kamat, in a grotto nearly a full day's climb up the slope," Ramapee explained as they settled down to a late supper of thick soup and coarse bread, served by an elderly couple, the cottage's caretakers. "Some consider him the greatest of the gods." A little smile lifted one corner of her mouth. "He is the god I serve so naturally I hold him in high esteem."

"Naturally," was Xit's dry response. "Every god has his good points. Yes, even Asak, your deity of death and darkness."

"But he negates all that is!" protested the priestess.

"His very existence prevents him from so doing," said the wizard. "Only the Void, complete non-being, can negate what exists."

"Well, maybe so but I still don't intend to worship him. Anyway," she continued, "you must climb to that shrine tomorrow and allow our seer to dream."

"Then we must spend the night up there?" asked Marana.

"It is only necessary for Saj to go up the holy mountain. Our Cana was fairly certain, however, that both of you would wish to accompany him." She spoke this to Marana and Xit.

"We shall," replied Marana, and turning to Saj, said, "and don't you raise any objections."

~

"The fire spears are jets of burning gas that occasionally burst forth along the route," Ramapee warned them. "They are the only real danger. Unless you fall off a ledge or something."

"We shall try not to," responded Xit, and turned to the upward path. Marana and Saj followed behind. They were more than willing to let the little wizard take the lead.

If wizard were exactly what he was. Saj was beginning to wonder about that; prosaic and matter of fact he might be — and he prided himself on it — but he was surrounded by mysteries and magic.

"Take care if the ground feels warm beneath your feet," said Xit. "Then the fires will be close beneath and the spears might become a threat."

"How will we know if one, um, is thrown at us?" asked Saj.

"You will be dead," explained Xit.

"That's simple enough," Marana remarked.

But would Xit be dead? Saj wondered about that, too, and suspected the answer would not be at all simple.

The way was not difficult, though rather steep, turning to stairs at some spots, and the route well marked by carvings on the black volcanic rocks. There must be occasional maintenance of the path upward. The 'spears' they saw flash from time to time, well off their pathway, but none erupted near them. That they would face them again on their descent they all realized, but now they could recognize the sort of crevices from which they burst.

"This must be it," spoke Xit. It was mid-afternoon and their shadows were growing long. It will be cold up here tonight, thought Saj, briefly, before turning his attention to what lay before them.

A statue stood in a narrow grotto. No, not really a statue, simply a round disk of burnished metal, possibly gold, with stylized rays emanating from it. The sun, the emblem of Kamat, it was meant to be. That was apparent. "There does seem to be — power here," stated Xit. "Emanations of great physical power such as volcanoes or violent storms can open the doors between the worlds." He gazed upon Saj for a moment. "It is likely that you will dream here."

"If I don't freeze," replied the young Mur. His eyes flickered to Marana, standing gazing at the emblem of Kamat. No, she would not help keep him warm this night. Best there be space between them, he felt, though he was not certain why.

Xit leaned over and placed a hand on the ground. "No freezing here," he stated. "The earth beneath us is warm even if the air grows cold."

A cold supper was shared and then, wrapped in woolen blankets, the three slept. And Saj did indeed dream.

~

He seems dazed, thought Marana. Saj sat at the mouth of the grotto, staring out over the valley of the Cana. As she approached, he looked up, asking, "Are we ready to go?"

"If you are, Saj." He rose, wordlessly, and in silence they descended.

"It weighs on him," Xit whispered to her. "I can not guess what he saw but we shall learn in time."

The sky was clear and deep blue. A lone vulture could be seen, very high. Xit again led the way, but now they kept the distracted Saj between them. At times he stumbled, not seeming to notice where he placed his feet.

The ground is hot here, thought Marana. There were fissures beside their path and, sometimes, crossing it. A hissing noise — Saj marched on before her, paying no attention to anything about him.

"Stop, stop," she called and grabbed him by his belt. Fire shot from the ground no more than a yard before him. Saj would have walked right into it. Another 'spear' flared to the left of their pathway and then no more.

The young man stood blinking. "Pay attention, you foolish boy!" she rasped at him. Her heart was tumbling within her chest. What if she had lost him here?

Xit stared at the pair, from a little further down the path.

Saj's eyes focused. "You saved my life, didn't you?" What impulse led him to pull her into his arms at that moment and kiss her? The boy turned back to their way, saying, "Let's get going. I'd like to be at the cottage before dark."

They were. But along the way, Xit could not help breaking into inexplicable laughter now and again. And it was Marana who seemed wrapped in her thoughts through the rest of the journey downward.

66

13.

I think I understand better now, Saj told himself. It had taken some time to sort out all he had dreamed on the slopes of the holy mountain. The day-long ride back provided that. He was ready to speak to the Cana, speak of the futures he had seen.

She sat patiently in her private chambers, waiting for his words. He might as well begin. "A great river, I saw, even greater than the Chas, and a numerous people dwelling up and down its length, and across the breadth of its broad valley. They were Ildin, but they called themselves Lamans.

"But they had forgotten the Cana who guided them, mixed her memory with that of gods and then forgotten those as well.

"And I saw — I saw my own descendants ruling there." He turned to Marana. "I am to be the father of dynasties, and you, their mother."

That is sort of a marriage proposal, isn't it? he thought. No need to go into that now. Nor anytime soon, for that matter.

Lura sighed. "I see there is a great destiny tied up with these stones and it is not for me to stand in its way. I shall give you the Fire Stone, even if little was seen of my own future. It does seem I am meant to lead those who remain here of the Ildin across the mountains and into that valley."

"Perhaps I can come and visit you there some day," said Xit.

"That would be good, Crocodile. Before we are both forgotten."

Saj hesitated before speaking further. "There was more but I saw it — dimly, distantly. A terrible cataclysm, a shaking of the earth, a rising of great, inundating waves from the sea. War and the fall of empires. It was all jumbled."

"Were we there?" asked Marana.

"You know he can not see himself," Xit reminded her.

"This valley was ruined." He raised his eyes to the east, where the unseen volcano stood. "Fire rained upon it. But you had already taken your people to safety."

"Ah. None of this is soon, I take it?"

"In my own lifetime, I think," Saj replied. "I — I saw my sons in the midst of it." He avoided looking at Marana, but turned his eyes to their hostess. "Grown men, they were."

Lura nodded. "Then we have at least a couple decades. That is good to know. All this is good to know and far more valuable than I expected. I thank you, Master Saj, and I thank Marana and Xit." She bowed her head briefly to each. "As I have promised already, the Eye is yours. I shall have it removed from my rod and delivered to the Lady Marana. You and Xit, I suspect, would rather not handle it."

"That is gracious, Mec Lura," came Xit's voice, gently. "We thank you."

"The Eye was of no more service if we are to leave this place and Kamat's holy mountain. Its departure will serve to mark the change that comes."

~

It was Ramapee who came to them with the news. Her oval face was grave. "Osale has disappeared."

"Who might that be?" inquired Xit.

"One of the men here whom we trusted to travel beyond the valley for trade. It is feared that he was swayed by the reward offered for news of your party and has gone to tell those who seek you."

Marana was curious. "A reward?"

The priestess nodded. "Word has come to us of this. Both Lord Gawif and your father have promised gold. They know that you came in this direction for they found the body of one of Gawif's men. You slew him, did you not?"

"I suppose we did," Xit admitted. "We really should have made sure of the job and buried him."

"One of those choices we had to make," said Saj, and barked out a laugh at his own jest.

"Yes, boy, it undoubtedly was."

"I wonder how much I am worth," said Marana, the reward still on her mind.

"More than whatever they are offering," answered Saj.

Xit shook his head. "You have turned that business-minded lad into quite the gallant, Lady Marana."

"On the contrary," objected Saj. "I was speaking purely as a merchant, assessing her true worth."

"To this Osale, it would seem I am worth exactly what is being offered."

"And now," sighed Xit, "the noblewoman seems to have been turned to businesswoman."

Marana and Saj only smiled at each other.

~

"Do you know where you wish to go next?" asked the Cana.

"North," replied Saj, who took another nibble of soft cheese before continuing. They made good cheese here, of the sheep's milk. He had not had such since leaving Muradon. "I sense the Sky Stone there." He thought for a moment. "In the mountains, or near them."

"The blue Eye. Yes, it would be in the north."

"And that will be the third," Xit said. "May they all be brought together again soon."

The look Lura gave him suggested she found his words most dubious. "It is not so long since some thought them better scattered. Scattered to the winds that are part of their essence."

"I was told they were stolen from an image made by your people," spoke Saj. "The Ildin, that is."

"From the statue of Banat, yes. Know you of Banat?"

The young man shook his head. "Not a thing, my lady," added Marana.

"Banat is the Father of the Winds, he who brings the breath of life to man from the four corners of the earth. He sits in the middle of things, seeing all with his four eyes." Her glance went to the young Mur. "In a sense, he sees as do you, young master.

"Some believe him the father of Kamat. Some do not. I suppose it does not matter, what with them being gods. Indeed, both ideas might be right. Banat is lord not only of the winds but also the elements. The stones, when discovered, seemed to hold the power of the elements and craftsmen of old carved the gems from a single rough jewel."

"Old?" asked Marana. "How old?"

Lura looked to Xit. "Millennia, I suppose?"

"Many millenia," he replied. "They were crafted, revered, utilized, long before they came to the Ildin or were associated with one of their gods."

"I knew that not. But my own people were on the other side of the world, after all."

"I'll tell you about it sometime. If we have a sometime, sometime."

The sorceress smiled indulgently at his words and continued. "It is known that the powerful and very ancient wizard Im stole the Eyes from the statue of Banat. But he did not long hold them."

"He found them no longer useful for his sort of magic," interjected Xit. "Which was not that much unlike my sort of magic."

"Yes, thieves the both of you. He traded them to some other mage. I don't remember the name." She glanced again at Xit but he offered no help with this. "It doesn't matter. But there was a, ah, trickster god, whom I shall not name here, who felt that the Eyes should not be together right then. He was one who could change his form and walk among mortals, this trickster."

"They offered too much power for any wizard who then lived to possess," Xit stated, rather emphatically. "Go on, my dear."

"I shall, Crocodile. So he stole them and scattered them about this land. It may be true that the Eyes are better off in the hands of those who do not use them for magic."

"They — amplify the powers of sorcerers and, um, people like me, don't they?" asked Saj. "That's what it seems like when I am near one."

"Focus, might be a better word," replied the Cana. "The Eyes may have no power in and of themselves." She then asked, "Have you touched the Fire Stone yet? I would guess that you are curious about it."

"I did put a finger on it, and then bade Marana to hide it away again. I must say that it didn't seem to have as much of an effect on me as the Earth Stone."

"The Earth Stone speaks more to your elemental make up, Master Saj," Xit told him. "You are very much of the earth, of money and prosperity." He looked beyond Saj to Lady Marana. "Do you feel anything when you handle the Fire Stone, my lady?"

She nodded. "It is very faint. It is as though it hums in my hand."

"It speaks to her. There must be much fire in the Lady Marana," said Lura. "And that is with no gifts of seeing or sorcery. Imagine, girl," she continued, addressing the noblewoman directly, "what it must be like for those with powers. Keep the stones safe and don't let either of these two try to take them from you. 'Twould not be good for them."

"You kept one near you," Marana pointed out.

"On the end of a stick," came Lura's answer.

Saj had to ask, "Is it a good idea to give them to the priests of Munu?"

"There could be far worse guardians," felt Xit. "But they don't have them yet."

~

They had been riding, Marana and Saj. They must exercise the horses, she had told him, but he knew well that she simply loved to be on horseback. It was a good place to ride, that rolling valley, and one wild flower or another always seemed to be in bloom. Saj felt no great urgency to depart and was certain it was the same with his companion. Yet until he completed his quest, their life together would not truly start. He knew that.

The Cana called them to her, in her throne room, upon their return to her house. Xit was already with the ruler of the valley.

"Small bodies of armed men have been spied, sniffing about our borders. We are safe here," Lura assured them. "One would need an army to break into our valley. And you are safe as long as you remain."

"But we can not remain," stated Saj.

"You could if you wanted, lad," Xit told him. "If you must continue your quest, you could pick it up again in a couple years."

The Cana laughed. "I thought you wanted the Eyes brought together, Crocodile!"

"There is plenty of time for that."

"For you, perhaps, and me. These two youngsters must rush toward their destiny."

"Yes, I suppose they must."

The Cana rose from her chair. She held yet her staff of office, but there was only an empty socket where the Fire Stone had once shone. "You need not go west and face the danger posed by those men. There are other ways."

"The pass?" hazarded Xit.

"It lies near. The Southern Pass through the mountains and into the great river valley beyond. I and my people shall follow you through that pass, one of these days and not return. You, however, might travel north on the other side and come back into Sharsh there.

"I shall provide you guides. Prepare yourselves to travel in three days time." She turned to Xit. "I shall miss you, my trickster," she spoke softly. "Return to me again sometime. And tonight, of course."

14.

By rugged paths they went, along ledges and through narrow canyons. "There are easier approaches to the pass," explained their guide, a lithe Ildin man named Torbo. "But they would take you nearer those who seek you."

The horses had to be led. All five they brought, all five they had taken into the Cana's valley, including Marana's fiery Ri. Him, she had to make certain to lead herself, occasionally giving him a reassuring word or pat so he would not become testy and take a bite of anyone.

'Anyone' included, besides the three and their guide, a pair of the Cana's soldiers. "There are wild beasts up here," one told them. "Your horses may get skittish if they scent a bear or panther."

"I would be grateful for the warning," Saj replied.

"Oh, they won't bother us. We are too many."

"Maybe at night," spoke his comrade. "One might try to get at a horse then. We'll need to post a watch."

"True enough. But we're safe in daylight. I don't think a dragon has been spied up here in years."

"Wild men are more of a danger than any wild animals," said Torbo, who had fallen back to join their conversation. He knew more of these mountains than did the soldiers, for he had often traversed them. "Perhaps those who are not quite men, as well."

"Trolls?" asked one soldier.

"And ogres and kobolds and dwarfs and who knows what else. They live up here to get away from our kind and don't always appreciate it when we come visiting. But usually," he added, "they just hide from us."

"I hear they can be partial to a bit of horse meat," the first soldier said.

"And other kinds of meat too," replied the other.

"I wouldn't worry too much about that," the guide told them, and returned to the head of their party. "We need to turn to the left up here and should reach the main way through the pass by dark," he called.

~

They camped beneath high rock walls. It was cool but not cold; summer still lingered though not much longer. "It never snows enough here to close the pass," the guide had said. "For that matter, even the Northern Pass usually remains open through winter."

The evening meal done, one soldier stood guard a little way from the fire; the other two Ildin slept, wrapped in woolen blankets. Yet the trio of travelers sat still by the embers.

"Are you a god?" asked Marana, suddenly. The same question had been in Saj's mind but he had so far kept himself from voicing it.

"Possibly," answered Xit.

The girl turned to Saj. "He would have to be a Baxac god, wouldn't he? I don't know anything about them."

"Me neither. Maybe that is just as well." He knew that would not satisfy her. "The only one I know of is Munu, whom the priests of the cave served. And they said he is not really a god at all."

"Munu is the best sort of god, boy," spoke Xit, "for he is in everyone and everything."

"But is there more of him in some than others? I sort of got that idea from Kambak."

"Some believe that. Some believe they can gather more of his power to themselves." For a moment it seemed the little wizard — or god? — would say no more. "I would say some simply recognize the essence of Munu that is already within them better than others."

"So we are all Munu?" asked a slightly perplexed Marana.

"Indeed. Therefor, we are all gods and I can answer your question by saying, yes, I am a god." Xit chuckled, rolled over, and went to sleep.

"I still think he is a god," Marana whispered and put her head on Saj's shoulder.

~

In places they could have ridden now, but their escort had no mounts. Saj chafed at their slow progress. Not that he truly needed to hurry anywhere but he knew it was in his nature to want to get on with things. He needed to watch that in himself.

Marana was all stop-and-go, full of impulses, where he was steady. No doubt each frustrated the other on occasion. But no sharp words had passed between them. Saj was enough of a realist to know that would not always be so; everyone slipped up sometime. They were doing well so far.

In time they reached the divide, crossed over and made a slow descent into the broad valley beyond. It was all forest of pine around them here, tall trees in a land that had never know the woodman's ax. Was it hotter on this side of the mountains? Perhaps being so far from the sea would have that effect; Saj did not know and was willing to admit as much.

"It is a lonely country, isn't it?" Marana asked one night. Thin clouds drifted across a waning moon. "Would anyone want to live here?"

"A farmer might," he replied. "There is land for the taking, with no nobleman to say it is his."

"Hmm. That will come, won't it?"

He laughed aloud. "Indeed it will. It always does."

"Is there land for the taking on Lorj?"

Saj realized that he wasn't sure. "I do know that great estates have been established in the north of the island, land worked mostly by slaves." Probably granted by the Viceroy or others high in the government to those with money and influence, he thought.

She wrinkled her nose at that. "It does not sound like a very good place to be."

"No. But I'm not really interested in any more land than is needed for a good house. Living quarters above, business below." He had laid out the plans for that house in his head many times.

"In Matanas?" That was the capital of Muram Lorj, after all, the home of the Viceroy.

"Maybe. Or one of the Ducal Cities. There are three or four of them down the coast."

"And you will own many ships and trade with the Southern Isles, right?"

"Exactly," said Saj. "You know my mind as well as do I."

"Better," she replied. "How else can I be a good wife to you?"

"Hush," he told her. "Not until the quest is finished."

"Then I shall simply kiss you now," said Marana, who did just that, and turned to sleep.

~

"We were told to return as soon as you safely reached this side," said one soldier, sounding slightly apologetic.

"We knew that. Fare home safely," Saj told him. "You as well," he said to the other, "and my thanks to both of you."

"And to the Cana," added Xit. "Be sure to give our thanks to her."

"We shall, sir. Well, we should be on our way." Both men at arms turned and began the trek back up to the pass.

"We can ride now," spoke Marana. "I am terribly sick of walking."

They could, indeed, placing Torbo on one of the extra horses. "Have you traveled frequently to the Northern Pass?" Saj asked the man.

"Admittedly, no," was the reply. "I've had no reason. There is very little on either side of the pass."

"That is why we are going this way," said Xit. Which was quite true.

The country they traversed as they turned north was still rugged. There was no reason to leave the foothills and travel further toward the great river they knew lay to their east. "There are settlements of my people here and there," Torbo informed them. "More in the south than elsewhere. The greater part of the migration came around the southern end of the mountains rather than through the passes.

"Another people is scattered in the north," he went on. "I do not understand their language; it sounds like neither Ildin nor Sharshic to me." The man turned to Saj. "I think they might have been displaced by your race a few generations ago."

"It is possible," replied Saj. There had been a native people, though not numerous, in his country before the Mura had landed. It was said that much of their blood remained in Arolin.

"They are fair people, lighter than you and I," continued the guide. "But usually dark of hair. Not unlike our lady." He nodded in the direction of Marana.

"My ancestors certainly didn't come from Muradon," she stated.

Saj shrugged. "Folks get around and often leave some of themselves behind."

"Most true," Xit said. "You two almost certainly have common ancestors if one goes back a way. And not as far back as you might think." He smiled at a sudden thought. "And you, Saj, are most definitely related to the Cana. All sorcerers in this world have the same ancestor."

"Does the Cana know this?" asked Torbo.

"I am certain that she does. It is part of the lore of her people."

They saw one of those natives, briefly, watching them before he disappeared among the pines. Or she, it might have been; it was too far to tell. No one offered them either welcome or mischief.

Much wildlife they saw, as well, and large, heavy-bodied birds that foraged beneath the trees fell more than once to Saj's sling. Torbo carried a bow but chose not to take a shot at the deer they occasionally glimpsed. "It would take too much time to dress one," he explained. "Also, the people who live here might not approve of us taking the larger game."

There were weeks of travel and autumn was in the air before Torbo turned them again toward the mountains. "The Northern Pass is undoubtedly the easiest route over the great mountains," he said, "considerably easier than the southern passage. Someday, perhaps, there will be reason to use it but now it is little traveled. The Mura do not even bother to guard their side."

"I don't think we really control the land over there," said Saj. "It is wilderness. But," he added, turning toward the west, toward the mountains, "there is something over there we need, and not too far away, I think."

"You sense the Sky Stone. Near?" asked Xit.

Saj nodded. "Very near. It is just across the peaks." He gave his companions a somewhat weary smile. "I would not be at all surprised if I dream of it tonight."

SETTING IV.
THE SKY STONE

15.

"It is in a sword. That I saw — a big, blue stone set in the pommel. I think its owner has no idea what it is."

Saj hesitated, seemingly perplexed. "And I saw a bird of some sort. Why, I do not understand."

"A black bird?" asked Torbo. "With white upon its wings?"

"Yes, yes, that is it." He looked at the guide questioningly.

Xit was likewise puzzled. "A magpie?"

"The bandit," stated Marana.

"So I would think," replied the guide.

"Magpie is an outlaw who operates from a base somewhere near the mountains," Marana explained.

"Some call him a bandit," said Torbo. "Others call him a fighter for freedom. A rebel against the Mura."

"I don't care what they call him," spoke Saj. "I just want the Sky Stone and he has it, I would be guessing."

"As it happens," Torbo went on, a bit hesitantly at first, "I know the Magpie and I know that sword you mentioned. We have dealings with him, the Cana does, that is. We're both outside the Muram law, so to speak." He sighed, resigned to his new course of action. "I meant to take you only through the pass and then return. But I suppose I really should introduce you to the man. Otherwise, he would be likely to use you as archery practice first and ask questions later."

"Being shot would be inconvenient. We would certainly welcome an introduction, Master Torbo," said Saj. "And — you had best introduce the lady as my wife." He turned to Marana and Xit. "Shall we use the same aliases as in the court of the Pretender?"

"We might as well," spoke Xit. "But why in the name of the Demons of Droga would we be here?"

"Poor Tom and his Bela have been driven from their homes by their harsh Muram masters," offered Marana. "We wandered across the mountains and were lost in the east until this kind Ildin found us and brought us here."

"That works," said Saj.

~

"Your Marana has read too many romances," muttered Xit in Saj's ear.

"Undoubtedly. It makes up for me having read none." My Marana, he thought. I like that.

It took a couple days to climb the rest of the way to the pass and now more than that had been spent descending. There was a road of sorts, a path overgrown with grass, leading further down into Sharsh.

A voice from the shadowed forest to their right. "Hail, Torbo! We did not expect you."

"I did not expect to be here, either, but circumstances brought me. I found these poor fools wandering on the other side of the mountains and knew not where else to take them."

"Wouldn't your queen take them in?"

"Magpie was far closer. And they seemed, ah, more his sort."

"He'll be the judge of that, I reckon." The man had stepped out onto the trail. That more remained hidden seemed likely. He was somewhat nondescript, bearded, in a grimy kilt, perhaps once plaid, and a leather vest. He held a bow, an arrow nocked.

He turned and waved to the woods. "I'll take them in," he called. "Unmounted," he said, turning again to the travelers. "And blindfolded."

"They always do this," explained Torbo in a low voice, "even though I know the exact location of their camp. And they know that I know."

Scarves were tied across their eyes; the bandit did not carry enough blindfolds so he had to borrow them from the Lady Marana. I hope Ri behaves through all of this, she briefly thought. It would not do for him to take a chunk out of our outlaw guide — and I can't keep an eye on him.

She did keep close to him, however, one hand on his mane, the other on the rope they all held to keep themselves on the path. It might have been as much as an hour they stumbled along before the bandit's gruff order came to remove their blindfolds. It was already growing dark. Before them, several fires lit up a collection of ramshackle lean-tos and tents.

They led their horses into the bandit camp.

~

It appears that we shall be speaking Sharshic again, Marana told herself. I shall have to take the lead.

The music of a flute rose from somewhere ahead of them. They approached a circle of ruffians gathered around a blazing fire. A tall man, not particularly young, and with a pot belly, stood to take a look at them. In his hand was a wooden flute. Was this Magpie?

Then he noticed her horse. "That is quite a steed, young woman."

"I stole it and made my escape on its back. He hated his master, too! Didn't you, Ri?" She stroked the horse's muzzle.

The old Sharshic name she had given the stallions seemed to make a favorable impression. She feared that she was also making too much of an impression on the outlaw leader.

His eye turned to her companions. "The boy is Muram," he stated, not exhibiting any emotion one way or another about the fact.

"Oh, the poor lad loves me and married me, despite his parents' objections. He is a bit simple, true, but he has always done his best." She could see that more than one of the men — and women — who now crowded behind their captain looked every bit as Muram as Saj. Magpie would apparently give any scoundrel an opportunity.

"And a Southerner."

Xit stepped forward. "I am just a poor runaway slave, great master. I may serve you, no?"

"We shall see. How name you yourself, boy?" He means Xit, Marana immediately recognized. Don't answer him Saj.

Oh, of course, Saj didn't understand Sharshic. Xit responded, "Xit, worshipful one! May I call you boss?"

"Magpie. Call me Magpie. We have no bosses here. Right, comrades?" A ragged cheer arose from behind him. "A company of equals, that's what we are."

Magpie's hair was sandy, mixed with gray, as was the tuft of beard on his chin. On one cheek, he wore three stripes of paint, black on either side of white. Marana had read that ancient Sharshite warriors had worn war paint. Perhaps Magpie had read the same book; no one living had kept up the tradition.

The same black and white emblem appeared on a tattered banner that occasionally unfurled a bit, when caught by the fitful evening breeze. No, it was a crudely drawn bird on the cloth, wasn't it?

"Your husband, you say," spoke Magpie, regarding Saj, who had been doing his best to look a simple farm boy. Not understanding a word spoken probably helped him with this.

"Yes, Magpie, sir. Have you a wife?"

"Do not call me sir. It doesn't really bother Magpie but my people don't like it. As for a wife, every woman here is my wife. We share and share alike in Magpie's band!"

Marana did not think highly of that idea.

The chieftain stood staring at them for a while longer. "Very well," he said, "welcome to the camp of Magpie. Make yourselves at home and we shall discuss things further on the morrow."

~

Saj quickly discovered he was not the only one in the camp who could not speak Sharshic. Much of the conversation around the fires was in Muram; it had, after all, become the common trade tongue all along the eastern shores of the Great Sea. The Muram he spoke, Saj knew, melded the many related languages and dialects that had originated on the other side of that sea into a new tongue. That those older languages were still in use in the kingdoms across the water, he also knew.

There were all sorts here, ranging from hardened criminals to runaway slaves to itinerant priests. These latter were of a cult with which he was unfamiliar, the Jevotes. Oh, he had heard things of them, and not good things — the religion was frowned upon and occasionally persecuted by the Mura — but Saj realized he actually knew nothing of their beliefs.

And many women, women of all ages. Many of these, too, were runaways of one sort or another. Some whores who had fled their pimps, some wives who had fled their husbands. Both sorts, and others, had found their way here, far from the centers of Muram power. Or any power.

"Magpie runs things with a light hand," one bandit told him. "But it does not do to cross him. We know who runs things even if he may say we are all equals."

"And he always gets the first choice of women," complained his companion, a squinty-eyed ruffian.

The first man shrugged. "They like him, for some reason. Even were he not chief, I think he would have no problem finding someone to warm his bed each night."

"Keep an eye on that young wife of yours," a third added. "He'll be sniffin' after 'er, that's a sure bet."

The other two nodded in agreement. "But he won't force himself on 'er," continued the bandit. "Magpie be a gentleman."

~

"I shall be on my way," Torbo informed him. "There is no more I can do for you here."

"Back through the pass?" asked Saj.

"No, it would be shorter and easier to go south. I know pathways that will keep me out of trouble." He looked toward the mountains they had recently crossed. "I know our Cana will soon be taking my people across. All of us knew the day would come. Perhaps we shall go as far as the great River Veltar that flows through that valley and settle beside it.”

“You have seen this river?”

“Yes, friend Saj, I have stood upon its western shore and could barely make out the eastern. It is a mightier river even than the Chas.”

“A part of me thinks it could be happy in such a place, away from strain and strife,” said Saj. “But it is a small part of me.”

“You a freeholder, a simple farmer? I can not see it. Marana, maybe, though she would have no one to order around but you. She is with Magpie?”

“Yes, and Xit too. They don’t need the dimwitted farm boy at that meeting.”

“That boy needs to keep an eye on them so they don’t get in trouble. Farewell to you, Saj.” The man turned and simply walked from the camp.

16.

"He played his flute for me," Marana reported.

Xit chuckled. "The man has extraordinary vanity. But he does play well."

"And we saw the Eye. He keeps the sword over there in his place." She waved an arm toward a ramshackle hut, one among several in the camp but the largest of the bunch.

Saj gave the hut a glance. "I don't suppose he might give it to us if we asked him."

"Not likely, even though he has no idea what it is," said Xit. "I'm not sure he even recognizes the Sky Stone as an actual valuable jewel, much less an object of mystical power."

"It is so large he might take it for no more than glass," added Marana.

"So we must steal it somehow."

"Or trade for it," spoke the noblewoman. "Maybe Magpie wants something we can give him."

"I do know he wants you, my dear," Xit said. "That is not for trade."

"Most definitely not," agreed Saj.

Marana sat in thought for a few moments. "I do not think he would take such a trade, anyway. As you said, Xit, Magpie is vain, too vain to trade for something he thinks he can win on his own." She giggled. "He would be insulted by the offer!"

"I think you are right. So what could he want?"

"Respect," said Saj. "To be more than a minor bandit lurking on the marches of the empire."

Xit nodded his head. "Well observed and quite true. But that is nothing we can give him."

"But we can certainly play to it," was the Mur's response.

A rawboned, freckled woman sauntered up to the group. "Bela, isn't it?" she asked Marana. "You need to get your things together and come bunk in our women's house. It doesn't do for you to be sleeping out here on the ground."

"I would rather be with my husband," the girl objected.

"Every man is your husband here," the woman stated loudly enough for anyone nearby to hear it. In a lower voice, she added, "That does not mean you have to accord them any wifely comfort. You need only be with the man you want."

"So — although I supposedly live in your, um, women's house, I could slip off and spend every night with Tom."

"You wouldn't be the only one with such an arrangement, dear," she said with a wink. "My name is Be." She looked over Saj and Xit. "You men should find arrangements too. There are spaces here and there, or you could build your own hut, if you prefer. So could you, girl, if you really don't like living with us. But do not, I warn you, share it with a man. That will only bring you ill will."

"Then I shall move in with you and your friends," declared Marana, gathering her belongings. "I suppose I can't keep Ri there."

The woman laughed. "I have heard of your Ri! No one is willing to get near him. I think, Bela, you could stable him pretty much anywhere you choose if it is away from the men and other horses."

Marana seemed struck with a sudden thought. "I shall be with you in a minute or two, Be. It's the big, um, house over there, right?" She pointed toward a hut with listing walls. "I need to discuss something with these two."

As soon as the woman left, Marana turned to the pair. "What if we gifted Magpie with Ri? A big warhorse like that would certainly make him feel a degree or two more grand. Practically legendary!"

"And what if Ri kills him?" asked Xit.

"Why then," said she, "we can take the sword of the legendary Magpie."

~

"Even in the rather short time the Mura have been on this side of the sea, their gods and those of Sharsh have become thoroughly mixed together in people's minds," spoke the priest.

That is certainly true, thought Saj. Though they conversed in Muram, he said nothing. He intended to continue playing his role of dullard around Magpie and the other high-ups in this band.

"But you believe in none of those gods," said Xit.

"There is but one god, Jev, who has created all."

"Ah, so he is not so different from the Munu of my people."

The priest obviously did not like his supreme deity being compared to any other gods. Before he could rebut this unsettling little fellow, Marana broke in with a question. "One god? How does he find time for everything?"

The Jevote had a ready answer, probably memorized from some catechism for just such times. "In that he created time, he would have all the time there is to act."

"Well answered," commented Xit.

"But who created your god?" asked Marana.

"Why, he created himself, of course."

"Obviously," added Magpie, "if he created all things."

The priest smiled approvingly upon his student. "Just so, Fonos."

Magpie scowled. "I gave up that name."

"It was given you at birth and Jev took note of it. Who are you to change it?" Magpie had no answer for this argument but did not look at all convinced. He fiddled with the flute in his hands. Magpie seemed to like having it with him.

Marana, however, did have something to say on it. "Can't he just tell Jev he changed it?"

"Yes, why not?" asked Magpie.

"Um, well of course Jev is all-knowing and is aware of this." The priest was at a loss for how to proceed.

"Then," said Xit, "he will recognize our captain, whatever name he might use. I have used other names on occasion, myself," he added, with a wink.

"I am not surprised," sniffed the holy man.

Marana turned to Magpie. The five of them were sitting in a circle on the ground just outside the bandit's headquarters. "Is all this sharing and equality you espouse part of being a Jevote?"

"I think it is. If Jev created all of us then one is as good as another, right?" He glanced at the priest, perhaps seeking approval.

"You know I agree," that man said. "You know also not all of our faith do."

"Humans are inclined to interpret all things to suit their own ends," spoke Xit, not sarcastically, but with a certain sorrow in his voice.

"Too true," agreed Magpie. The priest also solemnly nodded his head.

"But enough of this," spoke the bandit chief. "I must thank you, Bela, for giving me use of Ri. Of course, we all own him according to our rules but we would not have taken the horse from you." He chuckled. "Most would have been too afraid of him!"

"With good reason," she answered, and smiled sweetly. "I will help you make friends, Magpie, but it may never be wise to turn your back on the stallion."

Perhaps, thought Saj, men should fear Marana more than her horse.

Magpie but smiled in return and picked up his flute. "Let's have a song," said he, and raised it to his lips.

~

"Wake up, you two," said someone, shaking Saj. "It's time for you to go on your first raid!"

They had taken to lodging with several other men in a long lean-to on one side of the camp. No one bothered anyone else there; it was just a line of bedrolls under its minimal protection. Not the place to sleep in winter, Saj had noted. They would want to change quarters soon.

He sat up. There was a disorganized bustle in the camp, men rushing here and there, some leading horses. Saj turned to the Baxac wizard. "We are to finally become bandits, it seems."

"Not that either of us is much use as a fighting man," answered Xit. "Unless you have a sling in your hand, that is."

"You're a sling man?" asked he who had awakened them. "I'll remember that. Not much use to us today. It's gonna be horses and

88

swords and quick work if all goes well." He turned his eyes toward Xit. "You're on the puny side, aren't you? Any good with a sword?"

"Better with a knife," came Xit's response. "Preferably in the dark of night." He grinned wickedly.

"Ho! That also I must remember. I think you had best remain behind today, Brother Xit, but Tom will ride with us. Come and get a horse ready as soon as you are," the outlaw said, and left them.

"I do not like this at all," Saj told his friend. "I am no bandit."

"Most robberies consist of nothing more than brandishing a sword and intimidating ones victims," Xit told him. "I think you can do that."

The young Mur found one of the horses they had brought to the camp and saddled it. All the saddles were thrown together and it was essentially a matter of first come, first choice. This might actually be better than the one I brought, he told himself as he tightened the cinch. By the time he led his mount to the gathering area, Magpie had appeared, to the cheers of his followers, astride Ri and barely keeping the big stallion under control.

Some forty men thundered after their charismatic leader, and into the forest.

~

There couldn't be much to steal close to the camp. Just how far did they intend to ride? Saj had a reasonably good knowledge of where commerce flowed in Sharsh. Here, it simply didn't.

There were some manors in the upper Chas valley. That river turned north above the section he had rowed up with Marana and Xit, came closer to the headwaters of Indor, before looping back again eastward. Farm goods went across the hills there and down the valley to Indabas. But they were still far from even that area.

"It's the mines he's going for," said the man riding beside him. "There'll be gold coming down to the river."

"Aye, and plenty of soldiers to guard it," said another. "We have a fight ahead of us."

"Nay," spoke another. "Magpie's after the payroll for the lumberers."

"Maybe," allowed the first who had spoken. "I don't like stealing from honest workmen."

"Aren't the miners workmen?" asked Saj.

"Slaves, all," came the answer. "I'd like to ride into the mountains and kill those who drive them."

Saj found himself surprisingly sympathetic to that idea.

17.

"There they are now," spoke Magpie. "Exactly as expected."

There was a caravan on the road below them, several horsemen, baggage carts, a horse-litter at the middle of it all. A traveling noble or dignitary, most likely. Magpie must have spies to tell him of such things. Saj's estimate of the man and his organization grew somewhat at that moment. They had traveled nearly a week to intercept this little convoy.

Down they swooped on the travelers. There was little resistance; the armed footmen — who were probably no more than servants who had been asked to carry a spear — immediately threw down their arms. Two equesters saw the hopelessness of the situation and surrendered seconds later. The bandits surrounded their captives and booty. A woman thrust her head from behind the litter's curtains. It was Marana's mother, Lady Belema.

Saj tried to make himself as inconspicuous as possible, placing a burly bandit between himself and the noblewoman.

Too late. "Kidnapper!" she shrieked, pointing toward him.

"Tom!" bellowed Magpie. "Come forward!"

"Tom?" scoffed the Lady Belema. "That is Saj, the common trader who carried off my daughter."

The bandit leader looked from one to the other and burst into laughter. "Now here is a story Magpie wishes to hear!"

Magpie frequently referred to himself in the third person, Saj had noted. At first he thought it an affectation; on second consideration, he realized that the outlaw wanted to make sure his name was heard and remembered. Magpie sought fame.

Or, as he had himself suggested, respect.

Within half an hour, all of value had been stripped of the Sharshites and their horses and wagons were bound for the bandits' camp. Belema's litter was left sitting in the middle of the road, its horses gone with the rest. The Lady Belema and her people, however, were offered no harm nor were any taken away as prisoners.

"Ransom is too much trouble," one bandit whispered to Saj. "Even for someone as important as yon noblewoman."

It was undoubtedly good for Magpie's image, as well.

"Come here, ah, Saj, before we must end our business," ordered Magpie. "Have you aught to ask of this boy before we leave?" he asked Belema. The outlaw chief, true to his egalitarian ideals, refused to address her as 'lady.'

"Where is my daughter?" asked Lady Belema, more subdued now.

"Safely in Magpie's camp," he replied. "No harm has come to her."

"It was wrong of you to steal her."

"It has been suggested that she stole me, my lady. I am not quite certain." Saj felt rather weary, of a sudden. "Shall I carry any word to her?"

"Only that I love her, sir." She stared into his face for a few seconds. "Know that if my husband or Lord Gawif catches you, your death will not be an easy one." With that, she turned away from him.

~

Explanations were expected, when they camped that night, and were provided. Saj laid out all their story, but with no mention of the Eyes. To his surprise, however, Magpie knew of the theft of the Earth Stone.

Though he used not that name, saying only that he had heard a jewel had been lifted from the Pretender's crown. "I hope you got a good price for it," he said, apparently assuming they would have sold it for traveling money. Why hang onto such a thing?

"And you've been on the run since, eh?" Magpie shook his head in mock disbelief. "There is a reward for you, you know. And for, uh, Marana, right? I'll have to get used to that. I guess if I can change my name, so can she!" The outlaw chuckled at his little jest. "Not much mention of the little fellow, however."

He said no more of that until they returned to the main camp. Some of the booty was sent off elsewhere along the way, perhaps to be fenced.

Word of their identity immediately swept through the campground. This elevated them in the eyes of most there, and tales of their heist of Flawum's gem made the rounds. "We sold it to the Sorceress of the Mountains," Marana told anyone who wondered. "That's why her man Torbo was guiding us."

"It is fortunate that Magpie is not a suspicious man," Xit whispered to Saj, "or he would have questioned each of separately about our exploits and found some discrepancies."

"I believe he simply doesn't care," was Saj's opinion.

He did call all three to him, a day later. "One of our principles here," he told them, "is to question no one's past. Probably half the men here have lied about themselves to me, and I accept their stories. At least, I know you are not spies. For that matter, you have all the more reason to be loyal to our band, knowing that you are hunted in Sharsh.

"But," he continued, "you might wish to leave. That would be understood and permitted. Your enemies have an idea of where you are hiding. There are probably some around us in this encampment who would betray you for the reward. Not I, Sister, Brothers. But some."

Saj knew this was true. It did not matter, for their true objective had not yet been obtained — the Sky Stone. Until they had it in their hands — or Marana's pouch — and had a means of escaping safely, the three must remain.

~

"He sees me now as a bold fellow outlaw and is pursuing me all the more," complained Marana. "And playing that flute for me all the time! Magpie is the worst sort of romantic."

"Worse even than you, my lady? I did not know that was possible."

"You have been changing me into a practical woman of business, Saj."

"Never change all the way. That would be like marrying myself. Yes, yes, I know. I should not mention that idea."

"I shall forgive you. I think perhaps you have become more the romantic yourself."

"Maybe it is like Xit's Munu. These things are in us already and need but be discovered."

The pair strolled past the corral. "They still don't trust Ri with the other horses, do they?" asked Saj. "I don't see him."

"It will never be safe to put him with the others. Expect for an occasional mare, of course. I hear Magpie rode him well on your adventure."

"Well enough. He does not have firm enough a hand. But he fawns over that stallion as badly as you."

"Are you jealous, my Saj? Should I stroke your hair and whisper sweet things to you?"

"Just bring me the occasional apple. Ri gets all the best ones."

"I shall remember that! Will you ride again with Magpie?"

"He is bound to want me along on his forays. Perhaps I also am a 'bold outlaw' in his eyes." He put his arm around Marana. "But one not nearly as good looking.

"Before too long, Magpie will shift the camp," he went on. "Move to winter quarters. I would hope to have the Eye and be away before then.'

"Many things are to be hoped, Saj."

~

"The theory that has currently become popular with the philosophers is that there are but two elements, Fire and Substance."

"I must hold with the traditional four, Brother Magpie," replied Xit. "But I have heard this postulated."

"It makes a sort of sense," chimed in Saj. No longer having to pretend he was slow came as a great relief. It had taken more effort than he would ever have expected. "But if one believed in your Munu, Xit, wouldn't there be but one element making up all things?"

"And that element is Munu? Maybe so, Saj." He cocked an eye at Magpie and asked, "Or maybe it is Jev."

"No, no," objected the bandit. "The priests explained this to me. None of Jev's creation is equal to him so it must be of a lesser substance. Less complete." Magpie didn't sound completely sure he was getting it right.

"I know that argument," answered Xit. "It is the basic difference between my Munu and your Jev."

"I prefer my gods sitting atop the mountains and throwing thunderbolts," said Saj. "None of these abstractions."

Magpie laughed. "Then you are a devotee of Jov? You know the name is just a corruption of Jev."

"It's quite the other way around," Saj told him. "Anyway, Jov is the sort of god who won't bother me if I don't bother him."

"Then you do not pray?" asked Xit.

"If I knew a god worth praying to." Saj gave his friend a long, seemingly innocent look. But he knew Xit would understand what he was implying.

"There are none," replied the wizard. "They just can't be trusted."

~

She was nowhere to be found. Saj circumnavigated the entire encampment before going to Magpie. The bandit chief blinked for a moment in the early morning light as the information sank in.

"Assemble the camp!" he bellowed. "Everyone to me!" To a man standing near, his aide this morning, he whispered something and the fellow hurried off.

When his followers, somewhat over two-hundred strong, if one included a few children, stood before Magpie, he asked them, "Have any seen our sister Marana? And are any others missing from our band?"

"I haven't seen Sojel this morning," spoke one.

"I'm over here, fool," came an answering voice.

Someone asked, "Where is Kosh?"

"And Baggo?" called another.

The aide rushed up and blurted, "Three horses missing, Magpie!" A murmur rose from the crowd, an angry murmur.

"Traitors!" hissed a woman.

"They've gone for the reward!"

"They will get their reward," announced Magpie, "but not the one they desire. Assemble the riders!" He looked out at his people, the people who trusted him to lead. "They may reveal our location too, though not willingly. We must move camp immediately. All who do not ride with me get onto that task."

He looked about. "Sister Be, you take charge of that. Move them in small groups. You know the chosen spot."

"We shall watch for you there, Magpie," said she.

18.

Two men were hanging from a spreading oak by the roadside, their eyes staring at eternity.

"It's Kosh and Baggo," came a hushed voice.

"Aye. This was their reward," someone else spoke.

"They were tortured first," Magpie evenly stated. "I have no doubt they gave up our location."

Not far down the path, signs of their enemies' camp were found. "There were two bodies of men here," observed an outlaw. "One headed south and the other turned toward our camp. Soldiers those were, I think."

Magpie looked at the ground and nodded agreement. "Muram troops. We must depend on those we left behind to get away in time. Maybe forty men?"

"I would think so," replied the other. The Mura military was typically organized in groups of twenty. "A smaller party went that way." He looked down the road.

Magpie turned in his saddle to survey his troop. "We have more men but I've no illusions about their fighting skills. Those will be well-trained lancers ahead of us. Gawif's own guard, perhaps."

"And Gawif himself," added Saj, who had ridden close to the leader through this morning.

Magpie nodded an agreement. "Most likely." He shook his reins. "Go, Ri!"

The great war horse plunged forward and his troop followed. "It would be best to surprise them in a narrow space where they can not charge with their lances," said a man beside Saj as they rode on. "Magpie would know that."

"And he knows this country," Saj replied.

"That he does," agreed the bandit.

Within a few minutes, Magpie turned from the road. "We'll take them at Zalvo's Corner, I'd wager," said someone.

"Where better?" spoke another.

~

Two hours later, hours spent galloping over forested hills, Magpie waved at one of his lieutenants, and pointed to their right. The man immediately turned from the band, a dozen or more bandits following him. "They'll come at them from the front," was their leader's brief explanation. "And we from behind. We'll take them on the curve where they can not see both ways at once." They needed to wait but a few minutes before he turned and addressed his troop. "Quietly now, boys. Here they come."

A handful of men, carrying bows, dismounted and scrambled to a high spot Magpie pointed out. Down the road came the Sharshites. Twenty men, maybe, but all heavy cavalry, lancers, noted Saj. Where rode Marana among them? Which was Gawif? They were still too far away to tell. Below where they sat waiting, astride their horses, the roadway followed a turn in the stream that ran beside it. A steep hillside rose on the other side and by the water stood a small house, a crude sign declaring it a tavern. Zalvo's place, Saj assumed.

Behind it there appeared to be a water-wheel. Perhaps Zalvo was also a miller. Saj wished he had time to examine it; machinery ever fascinated him.

"Wait until they are at the corner, boys," Magpie muttered to himself. He raised a gauntleted fist, ready to give the signal. The men below them could be seen more clearly now and, in their midst, Marana. Her wrists are tied, Saj noted. Where rode Gawif?

Down came Magpie's fist. Down rained arrows and down came Magpie's troops, attacking each end of the little column. There was, indeed, no space for a lancer to charge. It would be sword against sword.

From the corner of his eye, Saj could see the archers rushing back down to their horses so they might join the fight. There would be no more arrows flying into that mass of fighting men. But one Sharshite had fallen from his horse and at least a couple others were wounded.

A fat man peeked from the entry of the tavern and then shut the door. A moment later he could be seen hurrying himself and his family, a wife and several children, across the low dam behind his establishment and into the woods beyond. A wise decision.

Magpie and Ri slammed into their opponents. The Sky Stone flashed in the pommel of the outlaw's sword, as it rose and fell.

A big man, not tall but immensely broad of shoulder, his torso protected by an ornate cuirass, charged toward the outlaw leader. A long white plume rose from his close helmet. Surely it was Gawif himself.

"I know that horse, scum!" he snarled, as he aimed a sweeping blow at Magpie's head. "He belonged to a far better man than you." Saj heard no more, for he was busy laying about himself with his own short, heavy sword. Thank Jov and Jev and any other gods for this shield, he said to himself, as he deflected more blows than he gave.

Magpie was hurt! He saw the man reel in his saddle, blood flowing from his side. He urged his horse to the outlaw's side, shielded him as he guided Ri toward the edge of the melee. Magpie still clasped his sword. "Take my blade, Brother Saj," he rasped, placing in it in the young man's hand. "Save your woman." He slipped from his saddle. Ri nickered softly and nuzzled his form.

"Guard him, boy," spoke Saj, and plunged back into the fray.

What was he doing? He was no swordsman. He could not face an accomplished slayer of men such as Gawif. Yet he drove toward him.

"Saj!" Marana cried. A warning? A cry for help?

Lord Gawif at her side. "So this is the Muram mongrel who took you?" The nobleman smiled grimly and spurred his mount toward him.

Saj lifted the sword of Magpie, ready to fight, ready, most likely, to die. Yet — he felt the power of the deep blue gem, the Sky Stone, set in its pommel. The Mur tried to keep it from distracting him as he deflected the first murderous blow from Gawif's weapon.

Then he knew. He knew he could *see* where the sword of Gawif would be, before it was there. It took some time to sort out those images in his mind, to learn to time what was to come, but he managed well enough to avoid the Sharshite's blade for a couple minutes of attack and parry. The man was obviously becoming frustrated, not expecting the youth to survive his onslaught.

He will swing the sword wide now, thought Saj, and lower his shield just a little to allow a freer movement of his shoulders. In went the sword of Magpie, a thrust into Gawif's throat. The man choked for a moment, then toppled from his seat.

It seemed that all those about him froze, gazing at what had just occurred, this unexpected end to a seemingly uneven fight. A cheer rose from the outlaws; those Sharshites still in their saddles turned and fled. None felt a need to pursue them.

~

Magpie was dead. Ri stood near, nibbling at the grass, and went peacefully with Marana when she took his halter in her hand.

Many men were dead, from both sides of the struggle. Any surviving Sharshites had their throats slit without ceremony; the wounded bandits were loaded onto their mounts and, last of all, the remains of their leader draped across a horse for his last journey. His last journey in this world — who is to say what journeys awaited Magpie elsewhere?

"You still have the Eyes?" Saj whispered to Marana.

"Gawif took them," she replied. "But I just took them back." The stripped body of the nobleman was piled with several others by the road. It was a poor gift to leave the innkeeper.

"We have another now." Saj held up the sword. "As soon as I can pry it from its setting, it would be best kept with the others." He was still seeing some things almost as a sort of double-vision, what was and what would be both at once. "In fact, you might carry the Magpie's sword back to the camp." He looked down the road. "If Xit had come along with us, we could be on our way right now and leave these bandits behind."

"But he didn't." Marana climbed onto Ri's back and reached down to take the offered sword. "So let us go where we must."

Most of the outlaws knew the way to their new quarters. It was further south, further west than the previous camp, a valley that would offer shelter through the months of snow. As they filed into it a couple days later, a solemn crowd gathered around Magpie's body and followed it into the center of the camp.

Be stood there, and Xit at her side. The woman spoke with a certain resignation. "I think we all knew Magpie would come home thus, someday. Though he himself, as a true follower of Jev, would have wanted his body cast aside as of no more value."

She went to the late bandit's form, now resting on the ground, wrapped in the cloak of some equally dead Sharshite equester. "I know a quiet place in the forest where we can leave his husk." Be looked down at the body. "Farewell, Magpie. You will be remembered as a legend." She placed his flute upon his chest.

"Did the Muram soldiers find you?" asked one of Magpie's lieutenants.

"They tried to and wandered about in the forest for a while. We took an occasional bow shot, just to remind them they could not come into our country with impunity." Be smiled with a certain satisfaction at the memory. "At last, they gave up and headed back west."

"More soldiers will come one of these days," said Xit. "That can be depended upon."

"And who will lead us then?" came a question from the crowd.

"Saj!" someone yelled.

"Saj! Saj!" came more acclamations.

At least momentarily, he had become a hero to these folk. But, of course, Saj had other places to go. What should he say to them?

Nothing, it turned out, for Marana stepped forward, Magpie's sword in her hand.

"We came to you through the Northern Pass, not long ago," said Marana. "There is a wide and empty land over there, beyond the mountains, a land free for the taking." She gazed from face to face of those gathered around her. "You could have the world you wish, live in peace and forget the nobles and wealthy merchants, the Muram overlords, their Sharshite lackeys. Magpie would have wanted you to live free.

"You could take them there, Be, come spring." She took the woman's hand. "Let Be lead you," she told the crowd.

They stood silently for a few seconds, thinking on her words.

101

"Why not?" asked one voice and "There's nothing for us here," spoke another.

"Be!" came a shout, and more followed.

"We shall depart tomorrow," Marana told the new leader of the outlaws, keeping her voice low. "We have a quest to finish."

"We shall miss you, Marana. And another," Be added, giving a long and rather fond look to Xit.

"I shall be ready to ride with you in the morn. But I think Be and I shall wish to, ah, say good bye tonight," Xit said, winking.

Evening was falling on the camp.

19.

"I am glad I kept the sword," decided Marana. "It is still a perfectly good blade without the Sky Stone in its hilt." She swung it a couple times. "It changed the balance a little." The young woman slipped the blade back into its scabbard. "I didn't notice a thing handling the stone."

"What know you of sword play, my lady?" asked Xit.

"Very little, I shall admit. But the rudiments are simple enough, aren't they? You hit someone with the sharp edge and they bleed!" Marana laughed rather loudly at her jest, before asking Saj, "Have you seen the next one? The last one!"

"It is very far away. And by the sea. That is all I sense right now." He gathered what insights he had and said, "We need to continue going east. South, too, I think."

"A long journey," observed Xit. "We might be able to go by water part of the way."

Marana nodded. "We should hit the Chas or a tributary of it soon."

"Let us hope it is more navigable than the last river to which you guided us," Saj said.

Marana chose to ignore the jibe. "It won't be. And it would take us far out of our way before looping back toward the sea." She had seen maps.

"Would we ever be able to take to boats?"

"At least the last leg," felt Xit. "But that would take us right past Sarowhem, you realize."

"Well, we need not deal with that yet," said Saj. "Let's get back to riding."

They mounted up and rode on silently for a time; it was their third day on the road since leaving the outlaw encampment. "I didn't want to leave Ri behind," said Marana, not very loudly.

"You couldn't ride him all the way to Lorj," Saj reminded her.

"No, I suppose not." Her smile came wistful. "I hope he likes it beyond the mountains."

"He will help populate that land over there with fine horses," said Saj. "The founder of his own dynasty."

And soon, thought the young man, perhaps we too shall found a dynasty.

~

There were ancient forests along their chosen path; huge oaks had gradually replaced the sky-spearing spruce of the mountains. That sky could be glimpsed only now and then through their branches.

They did reach a large river in time, a wild rushing river, which could be forded without too much difficulty. There were a few cabins at that ford, where the folk spoke only Sharshic, and Marana traded for a few provisions and asked of any news.

There was little to be heard, this far from things. Yes, it was said some nobleman was murdered in the mountains. Hundreds of bandits had ambushed him. It was best to stay clear of the mountains was the consensus. Best to stay clear of all outsiders, especially those Muram soldiers who came through every now and again. Suspicious looks were cast in Saj's direction. What was a nice Sharshite girl like her doing with him?

As for Xit, they had simply never seen anyone like him before. But they were pretty sure they didn't like him either. Even if he could speak the old Sharshic tongue to them.

Indeed, they were told, if they continued on the road east from here — there was an actual road now — they would reach the Chas. And yes, there were boats there that could carry them further. They sent trade items down that road from time to time, down to the town that lay at its far end. Furs, mostly.

Across the river went the travelers. The way grew ever more settled as they progressed, east and south of east, along the road, and the travelers grew more apprehensive. Gawif might be gone but Marana's father still offered a reward for her. News of such things got around.

"It is starting to look civilized around here, Wife Bela," said Saj.

104

"Too civilized, Tom." Farm land was becoming more common than woods, and some of those farms were large manors.

"You know I prefer cities. All this riding about the countryside we have done should last me the rest of my life."

"Were you a city boy?" asked Xit, who had ridden ahead of them but managed to eavesdrop, none the less.

"No, friend Xit. I grew up in a small village. All I ever wanted to do was leave it."

"Well, here comes yet another small village," announced Marana. A handful of thatched-roof cottages stood before them. "Tell me, good dame," she asked a woman they passed in the single dusty street, "how near are we to the river?"

The Sharshite peasant gave them a suspicious look, which they might have deserved. Saj was sure they appeared thoroughly disreputable. "Half a day, my lady," came the response.

'My lady' — apparently Marana looked like a noblewoman despite herself. Well, that was not to be helped. And then, being astride a horse tended to elevate people's estimate of ones station.

She thanked the woman and passed on. "Close. I suppose we should sell our horses there." Marana patted her mare's neck. She did become attached to her mounts.

"We could ride all the way," said Saj, with noticeably little enthusiasm.

"No, I know that would slow us down too much."

"The distance is about the same either way," said Xit. "But the river seems both safer and faster."

It was near evening when they crossed a low ridge to behold a good-sized town along the broad Chas. "More than I expected to find at the end of this road," said Saj. "It might be a good idea to camp up here tonight and ride down in the morning."

~

Perhaps half a mile of buildings along the river could be seen by dawn's light, low buildings, and very little inland from them. Just one road paralleled the Chas. That road was dirt, they found, when they reached it. A high bluff lay behind the town, overlooking the river. That would be a fine place to build a fortress, thought Saj.

"What is this town named?" wondered Marana. "It wouldn't do to ask, would it?"

"It could draw attention," admitted Xit. "We should try to get out of it and on the river as soon as possible." They *were* drawing attention, already. "There's a tavern. Let's duck into there and see what is to be learned. And whether there is any decent wine to be had."

The inn was rather unimaginatively named 'Dog's Place.' "I like dogs," stated Marana and led the way in. It was a low-ceilinged room, with rough-hewn beam and post construction, and stuccoed infill. The barkeep — if he was 'Dog,' he must be one of the smaller breeds — did not give them much of a look. All sorts would show up in a town such as this.

Xit spoke lowly with the man, handed over a few coins, and brought tumblers of a brownish wine to their table. "We can sell our mounts right here, if we wish, and buy a boat too. Dealers in both come in and out." He glanced toward their host. "Dog, no doubt, gets a cut."

"Buy one? I thought we would take passage," spoke Saj.

"We can be less conspicuous this way. We might want to hide by day once we get downriver a bit." Xit sipped of his wine. "Truly a reprehensible vintage." He drank on.

Noontime found them at the river, gazing on a small boat. "At least it is bigger than the one we stole from your father," said Saj. "Are you sure it will do, Xit?"

"It should. Ready to go?"

Marana was surprised. "Right now?"

"Why not? We paid for it, our gear is here, our horses are sold. Let's get out of this place." Xit surveyed the makeshift buildings along the waterfront. "This town will never amount to much," said he.

Saj was not so certain. He tended to see potential everywhere. No matter. "Get aboard, you two, and let's be off!"

~

The Chas was already a large river at the town where they had launched. It grew larger. Quite sizable boats made their way up and down the stream, some fitted with sails, most oar-driven. Saj suspected even a ship like Captain Sokor's could make its way up into these reaches of the river. The travelers had been assured they were below any falls or rapids.

Lumber barges were passed by occasionally. Those had come from even further upriver, from forests such as those through which they had journeyed. "There might be money in timber," mused Saj, killing the time with whatever conversation he could.

"Lots of cypress down in Lorj," answered Xit. "Most of it stays there. You'll see it in construction when you finally make it to the island."

"You will use it to build us a very large house," Marana said. "Living quarters above, of course, and offices below. And," she continued, "you must add a stable."

"Should it have mosaics?" asked Saj.

"It does not matter as long as there are horses. And dogs. We must have dogs."

"Oh," said Saj, "two large and very vicious guard dogs will remain on the bottom floor when we retire for the evening."

"But the children will sneak down and make pets of them," Marana decided.

Saj chuckled. "I know you would, anyway."

"For two people who refuse to discuss marriage," observed Xit, "you certainly skirt all around the subject."

In a surprisingly short time — at least to Saj's mind — they passed by the side-stream where they had turned toward the Pretender's lands. It would not be that much further to Sarowhem. "We should switch to travel by night," he told his companions. "I'm going to pull over right now and wait for sunset before continuing."

Xit nodded his approval and helped paddle toward the southern bank. They pulled their boat up into concealment and prepared to nap a few hours.

And were awakened by a voice that seemed familiar to Saj. "This seems a good spot to camp." He opened his eyes to see the High Priest Kambak and two of his followers.

Saj immediately had his short sword at the ready. "Tush, young man, we mean you no harm," chided Kambak, holding up his hands. "Nor could we do you any if we did mean it. We are three soft old priests to your three hardened adventurers."

"Greetings, Kambak," spoke Xit. "This is the Lady Marana, as you would have guessed."

"Greetings, my lady." The High Priest bowed in her direction. "And greetings to you, Xit. I suppose it was your idea to change the plans we made."

"This way seemed better. Certainly better for these two."

Kambak shrugged. "It matters not, if we obtain the Eyes in the end." He spoke again to Saj. "You have gathered three now? That is what we would guess from the reports we have received."

"I knew you had spies, old man," muttered Xit.

"That is how I guessed you were here, my dear Xit."

Saj answered the priest's question. "Yes, three. And we shall retain them until we have gathered all four. This I promised to do."

"I believe you, Master Saj, and know you to be an honest man. Nor would I expect you to give up any of your bargaining power at this point," Kambak added, the ghost of a smile on his dark face.

"Moreover, were I actually able to wrest them, or the Lady Marana, for that matter, from you, I know you would refuse to go after the fourth Eye. So it will be. Know that I have one more thing to offer you as a reward when you gather all four stones — we have a ship and can take you with us to Lorj, where our order has its home."

The priest of Munu looked from one to another of the three. "Good enough? Very well, if business is over, let us eat."

"I do not believe we will get back onto the river tonight," Saj whispered to Marana.

"I just hope they brought their own food," she whispered back.

~

"Tell me, your holiness," said Marana, after a quite satisfying meal provided entirely by the priests, "does a crocodile appear in the sacred traditions of your people?"

Xit clearly disapproved of the question but held his tongue.

"A most interesting inquiry, young lady! Yes, there are those who believe the first men descended from a crocodile," he began, "but that crocodile was in truth the trickster god Xido, who could change his skin. Xido still walks among men from time to time, it is said."

"A trickster god, you say? That is intriguing."

"Only a myth, of course," continued Kambak. "The old gods are but metaphors for the many aspects of Munu in the universe."

Xit sounded as though he were choking.

"That is too bad," said Marana. "He would have been interesting to meet."

Setting V.
THE SEA STONE

20.

"If Kambak could find us, then so might Hurrum."

They had laid low the entire day after the priests of Munu left them, paddling their own canoe downriver at dawn. Saj chafed at the delay.

"All we can do is take care," said Marana.

"I think it will be safe enough to slip past your home —"

"My parents' home," Marana interjected, quite emphatically.

"Yes, your parents' home," Xit went on, "under cover of dark. I can even pull in a little shadow on us. Or fog. Yes, fog would be good. At any rate, if your father had any idea where you were he would already be here. He certainly would not wait for you to float by."

That was true, felt Saj. A few nights later they did float silently by Sarowhem, mists all about their little boat. Marana watched the shore slide by until her former home had disappeared.

"It is going to be harder to hide by day, further down," she said after a while. "There are many estates along the river, until one reaches the swamp regions."

Saj knew the mouth of the Chas was a low, wild land, where few men lived and no civilized ones. There was no port down there; one had to come some ten leagues upriver to dock. "Some good-sized towns too, aren't there?" he asked.

"Yes. We will need to stop somewhere for provisions unless you two catch enough fish."

"I have eaten far too much fish in my lifetime," was all Xit had to say about that.

"So which of us is best suited to go ashore and buy something?" asked Saj. He took the occasional leisurely stroke with his paddle, more to keep the boat headed the proper direction than to propel it. The current was taking care of that.

"I am," Marana answered. "I am both the most knowledgeable of the area and the least recognizable."

Xit agreed with this. "One of the bigger towns would be better, where many come and go."

"Yes." The girl nodded somewhat absently. "How much further must we go down this river?"

"To the sea, I think," replied Saj. "I have not yet seen the stone but I am sure it is by the Great Sea somewhere."

"That is not too surprising," said Xit.

~

There was more traffic on the Chas down here. It might be safe just to blend in with the other boats. Who would notice one more?

They did chance a daytime visit to a town and waited anxiously while Marana visited the market, barefoot and in a shabby gown, a shawl about her shoulders. Who would take her for a noblewoman like that? She returned with meat and bread and vegetables and even a jug of wine. "We could pull over to the bank tonight and have a fire," she suggested. There was a pleading note in her voice and, in all honesty, the men liked the idea of a hot meal and fire.

And that night, Saj dreamed. "I have seen the Sea Stone," he announced as soon as the others awakened. "A great green gem set into a cup or goblet. Of silver? It didn't quite seem to be." He sat, sorting through what he had seen. "A women held it. A Muram woman, I think, and she raised it in a toast. There were many men there, hard-looking men, and — the sea. They were by the sea. I think that is all."

"The Pirate Queen," spoke Xit, in a rather small and discouraged voice.

"So you think?" asked Marana. "That thought came to me too."

112

"Isn't that but a legend?" came from Saj, as he looked from the one to the other.

"Tell that to her many victims. Those two galleys you encountered might have been hers. It is said," continued Xit, "that she has a base somewhere near the mouth of this river, concealed in the swamps."

"The navy has been unable to rout the pirates out," added Marana. "My — my brother disappeared when he served on an expedition against her and her men."

Saj had heard rumors most of his life that the Muram navy took a cut from the pirates' loot and let them operate as they would. Not so long ago, that navy itself was little more than a pirate fleet, raiding the coasts of Sharsh. It would not do to bring this up right now.

"Very well," he said. "Pirates, I can believe. But a queen?"

Xit chuckled softly. "She is Muram. You know Muram women, boy."

Saj did, indeed. "We shall have to find some way of dealing with her when we get there," was all he could say.

~

"There are horsemen on the north bank," said Marana. "They have been staying abreast of our boat."

Saj and Xit looked to their right. Yes. The river was very wide here but they could make them out. They had been there earlier, thought Saj. They were obviously keeping an eye on the boat.

"We must have been recognized," the noblewoman went on. "Maybe someone saw me in the market and made a connection. Perhaps a passing boatman put things together."

"We can be certain there will be boats in pursuit of us soon," warned Xit. Small galleys patrolled the lower Chas.

"It won't do to pass by Azer," Saj said, that being the large port town that lay some distance up the river from its swampy delta. "It would be best to get off the river altogether, right now." There was no need for further discussion; all three paddled hard for the southern shore of the Chas. "They will try to cross and be after us as soon as they are able."

"Unless they take the extra time to come over in a barge, they will not have their horses," said Marana. "They will not have that advantage."

Horses would have been of no advantage, anyway. The south side of the Chas proved very marshy. "There," called Xit, pointing to a channel. Through the reeds and tall, coarse grass they half-rowed, half-paddled their craft. "It will be impossible to find a way through here," he said, "for both our pursuers and ourselves. How are we to finish our journey to the sea?"

"I don't think we can walk," Saj replied, "and we shouldn't return to the river. Damn, the bugs are pesky!" He swatted at something biting his arm. "I wouldn't have wanted to venture onto the Great Sea in this little boat, anyway."

"A good point."

"For now," suggested Marana, "why don't we get ourselves well hidden in case someone comes into these marshes after us? We can decide our course later."

Xit's chuckle was barely to be heard above the din of buzzing insects. "Saj is the one who is supposed to come up with such practical thoughts. That is indeed what we should do."

They maneuvered their vessel into as hidden a spot as they could find and lay down, covering themselves with cloaks, as much to protect from mosquitoes as to hide them. Once they heard voices at some distance, calling, and others answering from a different direction. After darkness fell, Saj thought he once caught the glint of a lantern, far off.

"They are not likely to give up," whispered Marana. "They know we are here somewhere. Do you think we could find our way back to the river? We could drift down and escape in the night."

"Another good plan," felt Xit. "Shall we, Saj?"

"Better than sitting here and being eaten alive!"

"Try to follow the flow of the water. It must lead back to the Chas eventually," advised Xit.

It did, and much more quickly than any had expected. "I thought we might wander in those reeds forever," Marana said, as their boat slipped out onto the dark river and toward the sea.

"They will not follow right away," said Saj, "but they will be after us again soon. And there will be those watching for us further down. We shall have to again leave the river, and soon."

"Yes," agreed Marana. "We have escaped but word will now reach my father."

~

With the first faint light of dawn, they again pulled to the southern bank. "I believe this is as far north as the cypress grow," remarked Xit, looking up at a tall specimen. "The marsh is giving way to swamp." The boat was rowed far back among the trees and pulled onto a low island. "Watch for snakes," warned the wizard, quite cheerfully.

They were all a bit more cheerful now. Had they not escaped danger once again? Saj stood on the sandy shore and found himself drawn to gaze southward. "It is there," he said, pointing.

"Straight south?" asked Xit. "Perhaps we could come close traveling through these swamps."

"Or become thoroughly lost," commented Marana.

Xit shook his head. "Nay, our Saj is as good as a lodestone. He will ever point toward the stone we seek." He looked around. "Yet we are only at the edge of the swamps. Perhaps another night's trip further down the river would be wise."

"No." said Saj, turning back to his fellow travelers. "We go further into the swamps and we go now."

They offered no objections.

21.

Dreary day followed dreary day. There were blind ways where they must turn and retrace their route, yet progress was made, slowly.

There were people in those swamps, some dwelling in shacks on pilings above the water, some in shacks on bits of higher land. It was assumed there were people, for they saw those shacks. Of the people they saw nothing.

That was just as well. The travelers had no desire to make themselves known. The high crowns of the cypress, shrouded in hanging moss, allowed a half-light to filter into the world through which they passed. They were both alone and surrounded by life. Scarlet bromeliads bloomed above them. The great black and white woodpecker's laughter echoed in the distance. Below, the water swarmed with fish and with turtles. Snakes swam or slithered by regularly, and otters gamboled on the shores, diving into the dark water only when they approached too closely.

"I know not whether any sort of crocodile can live this far north," said Xit. "There might be a few in this swamp, shy and hidden."

"The water flows more swiftly here," Marana observed one day, a day that had seemed like all the others. How many had they spent paddling through the gloom, now?

"The are several smaller channels through which Chas reaches the sea, in addition to the main flow. Perhaps we near one of those," conjectured Xit. "But we might not want to enter it."

"That depends on whether it flows toward our objective," said Saj. He peered at the shoreline they were paddling by. "I have not seen trees like those before."

Xit followed his gaze. They were small, little more than shrubs, with exposed roots and shining dark green leaves. "Those are mangrove," he said. "As with the cypress, we are near the northern end of their range. They grow near salt water." He thrust a hand into the water and licked a finger. "Brackish."

They saw more mangrove, though they were scarce. This was, indeed, the northern edge of their range and they did not seem to prosper here. However, the cypress began to give way to thickets of scrub and grassy marshes. Even an occasional pine rose from bits of higher ground. Saj could smell salt in the air.

A cry from above. He looked up to see gulls wheeling. And was that the distant crash of waves? They emerged into a wider, almost lake-like expanse of water. A taste showed that it was quite salty. "Those are tide flats all about us," Saj told his companions, pointing to what looked like fields of grass. He had seen such frequently enough, around the coasts and river-mouths of Muradon.

"Over there," he said, and paddled for a sandy bank he had spied across the water, a higher spot amid the marshes. They pulled their craft onto the shore and clambered up to gaze upon a sand beach and, beyond it, the Great Sea.

~

"Where from here?" asked Xit, reclining by their fire of drift-wood. Surf of a somewhat modest size crashed in the darkness.

Saj shrugged. "I am not certain. The Eye is near is all I can say." He swatted and cursed. Mosquitoes did not seem to visit this beach but there were tiny biting flies that were, perhaps, even worse. "We might even have overshot it."

"If there is a pirate base, it would be back in the swamps, wouldn't it?" asked Marana. "Hidden?"

"That would make sense," agreed Xit. "Let's sleep on it. Who knows, maybe our seer will dream something useful."

Dreams proved unnecessary. Saj awoke to see a number of half-naked men standing about them, swords hanging at every waist. "We saw your fire," said their apparent leader, seeing that he was awake. "Shipwrecked, were you?"

Xit was awake now. He shook Marana. "On the contrary, sir," spoke Saj. "We are refugees from the law who escaped through the swamps." Which was essentially true. "Our boat is over there."

"Go look," the headman told one his pirates. For pirates they obviously were. No need to go searching for them!

"It is so," reported the man on his return. "Mighty little boat to be traveling in." It was growing lighter and Saj could make out their visitors — captors? — better now. Most looked somewhat Muram. Not all.

And their accents, although they spoke the common Muram of his own people, varied considerably as they discussed what to do with the trio they had come upon.

"I say slit the men's throats and enjoy the woman," said one, leering at Marana.

"None of that," admonished his leader. "They may be valuable. We wouldn't want to spoil the girl is she is to go to the slave markets."

"Bah, you think too much of profits."

"That is why we are in this business." The chief turned to the man he had sent to check the boat. "Is it worth taking with us?"

"I wouldn't bother, boss. It looks like they brought all their gear up here." He surveyed the travelers' meager belongings.

"Good enough." The headman turned to the three, his decision made. "Gather your things and come with us."

As they bundled up their blankets and bags, one of the pirates conferred in a low voice with their leader, both glancing their direction from time to time, the chief giving an occasional nod. Then he sauntered over to Marana. "You're that runaway girl aren't you? From some noble estate up the Chas. We've heard there is a sizable reward." He looked at Saj. "For you, too. I wouldn't want to be in your sandals if her dad got hold of you."

He shrugged. "But that's not for me to decide one way or the other. We'll leave what happens to all of you to Qala. Come along."

~

The pirates' vessel was small and light enough to draw up onto the beach. For that reason, Saj would have described it as a large boat. Another might have said small ship. Whichever, it had room enough to fit three passengers in along with the half-dozen crew. It was not on the wave-battered beach, exactly, but pulled in at the edge of a small inlet. Perhaps that pass through the sands communicated with the tide flats Saj and his friends had crossed.

But their hosts — Saj preferred to consider them such for now — did not enter it but launched into the sea, raised a sail, and headed south. A triangular sail, he noted. One of those he discussed with Sokor? There was little time to consider that as they soon turned the craft into another inlet. "Reckon we should blindfold 'em?" asked someone.

"Best to be safe," agreed their leader. "Safe from Qala, that is — she'd have our skins if we let them learn the way in!" There were hearty laughs from all around.

A bag was placed over each head. "It's hot, mate, I know," said the pirate who slipped a sack over Saj's head. "But better having your head in a bag for a while than losing it."

"Or your eyes," said another. "I reckon you'll find welcome at the Rock. By all accounts, you're a bold fellow."

"But Qala might not let you keep the girl," warned the first.

The darkness, the heat, seemed interminable. The pirates were rowing, not sailing, he could tell. Saj was also fairly certain they were in the shade of trees the better part of the time. How long? Certainly an hour, he felt, but maybe not much more than that. Then he was blinking in the sun, blinking at a squat fortress set on a rocky isle. All around was a wide lake. Probably salt water, he thought. There were several boats and ships of differing sizes moored about it, including a pair of long black galleys. He could make out buildings and docks along the far shore of the lake.

"The Rock," the headman announced, as he guided the boat in along a quay, part natural rock, part laid-up stone. He stepped ashore and conferred for several minutes with a heavyset man in a blue kilt. Again, there were many glances in their direction, before the fat pirate turned and hurried toward the keep and the chief turned his attention back to them.

"Come on ashore. I don't know if the queen will want to see you right away but we have to wait here until we find out." He gave the three another looking over. "Is it true you stole the Pretender's crown?" he asked.

"Only a gem from it," answered Saj. "The crown was too large to fit in my pocket." The pirates laughed uproariously at that.

"There are rumors you led an outlaw band in the mountains, too."

"There is some truth to that." Not much, but some.

"Don't expect to be a leader here. You may end up pulling an oar in one of our galleys. I'm doubting it, boy, but you might rub Qala the wrong way. One never knows."

"Qala is your, um, legendary queen?"

"That she is. The best leader we ever had, by which I mean the one that has brought in the most profits. Oh, she can fight well enough but that's not what is needed."

Saj nodded an agreement. Here came the heavy pirate, bringing some word on their fate.

"Bring them before Qala!"

~

Qala proved to be a surprisingly petite woman. She was, going by her looks, thoroughly Muram, and, going by her accent, from across the Great Sea. The hair was straight and black, the skin almost golden. Her hand caressed the hilt of a heavy curved blade hanging at her side.

"Word of who you are has reached even we who dwell here, hidden," spoke the Pirate Queen. She glanced past Xit to give his companions a rather frank and forward looking-over.

"Is she interested in Saj?" Marana whispered to Xit.

"No, my lady," he whispered in return. "I think she is interested in you."

"Oh!" The young noblewoman gasped, perhaps more in surprise than aught else. "This is even worse than Magpie!" She eyed their hostess. "Well, maybe not."

"You look to be a good Muram boy," said the queen to Saj, "and being on the run from a Sharshite nobleman is all in your favor. We prefer such as you in our ranks rather than at the oars."

"Your highness," piped up Xit, "the boy and I are sorcerers. He is, ah, my apprentice. Might we serve you somehow in that capacity?"

120

The woman looked with new interest upon the little wizard, and then turned to one the attendants. "Bring the cup!" she ordered. To Xit, she said, "Can you see what is to come?"

Xit gave a sidelong glance at his young friends and spoke. "There are those who have named my student Saj the Seer, your highness."

"Don't call me that," came her curt reply. "My name is Qala and that is good enough for me and anyone else. All the world trembles at the sound of it!" Qala laughed at their expressions. "Well, so I would hope. Ah, now for the test."

She took a cup of somewhat modest size from a black-lacquered box the pirate had brought her. A deep green gem shone, set into the silvery metal. "Once we had a shaman who could read things in this stone," Qala spoke. "Things of the sea. Our shaman could predict storms by gazing into its depths and sometimes see ships for the taking.

"The old fellow passed last year. If you have the ability, you will take his place." She was obviously telling Saj this, not asking him. Qala held it out to him. "Take it, boy."

Saj reluctantly accepted the goblet. Tentatively, he placed a fore-finger on the jewel. Not so bad, but he could feel its power. It was almost calming. He may have stood there, half-dreaming for some time, before he became aware of the queen's impatient stare. Did he see anything?

The sea. Not unexpected. Storms? Far away, but their energy flowed toward him, dark, heavy waves coming in his direction. For a moment, he shrank within himself, thinking they would engulf him.

"He has seen something," spoke a man positioned at the foot of the pirate leader's dais. Saj had noted that she allowed none to stand near her. "I remember that look on old Agos." Qala waited for him to speak.

"I saw only — waves, I am afraid. A large swell rolling from the northwest."

The Pirate Queen shrugged. "Agos rarely saw any better. An early storm of winter, you think?" she asked the man who had spoken, apparently her second in command.

"It is possible. We can find out if the lad speaks truth in a day or two." The pirate gave him an unfriendly look. "If you lie, boy, it is a chain and an oar for you."

"That is for me to decide, Jacef," said Qala. "Find these three some quarters and keep an eye on them."

"Platinum," Xit said, as they were led away. "The cup is of platinum. Worth more than gold but that matters little to us."

"At least the Eye will be in my presence from time to time. No one searched you, did they, Marana?"

"No, Saj, the other stones are safe for now. But maybe I should conceal them somewhere rather than carry them about on me."

It was not exactly a cell in which they were placed, but it was close, and a guard was posted outside the heavy iron-bound door. The stone walls were damp.

"This is not the healthiest of places to live, is it?" asked Marana. "The swamps must be full of evil humors."

"It is the creatures that dwell in these swamps that bring disease. The biting insects, the rats —" Xit suddenly noticed Saj sitting, staring into space. "What is it, boy?"

"The Eyes." He glanced toward Marana. "They are calling to the Sea Stone."

Xit stood still for a moment, as if listening. "They are, aren't they? Though calling is not quite the word, as they are not sentient nor even alive. But there is an — attraction, a force, that pulls upon them."

Saj slowly nodded. "Pulls them to again be one."

22.

Qala called them to her the next day to hear their entire story. Once again, they provided all the details except for mention of the Eyes.

"Most entertaining," she told them, at the conclusion. "I am even inclined to believe most of it." The queen turned to Marana. "The sword in your possession. That was this Magpie's?"

"It was, my, uh, I shouldn't call you my lady, should I?"

"Use my name, girl."

"Yes. It was Magpie's sword, Qala."

Qala turned to Saj. "But you used it to slay Lord Gawif, no?"

He nodded. "I did."

"Where is the stone from its pommel?"

"We had to sell it, Qala," spoke Xit. "We were low on funds."

"Yes, Xit gambles," confided Marana.

"Very well. Cash does seem to pass through your hands rather quickly. It is a common failing in our line of work." Qala again addressed Marana. "There was armor of a sort in your belongings."

The noblewoman blushed, despite herself. "Um, I was — given that by Flawum. The Pretender. He liked the way I looked in it."

"So might I. Some other day, perhaps."

She turned to Saj. "Through all your adventures, she has remained a virgin, has she not? Ah, you need not answer — your face does it for you." Her smile was smug. "I suspected this."

Marana's face was quite red, now.

"I was told you did not sleep together. None of you. Most curious."

"We agreed to wait until we were safely on our way to Lorj," blurted Marana. "Saj is going to be a successful trader there."

"He *was* going to be one. Now he is my shaman and he will not leave the Rock again." She fixed her dark eyes on the boy. "Assuming his promised waves show up."

Fortunately for all of them, there was a massive swell pounding the coasts of the Great Sea the next day.

~

"I would guess Qala to be in her mid-thirties," said Xit. "Maybe late-thirties. I've always found it difficult to tell with Muram women. And she has ruled here for a long time. Almost half her life, it seems."

"Why should that be of any surprise to you?" asked Marana, perhaps a bit more shortly than needed. The girl was not in the best of moods after their interview. "Can't a woman be a good leader?"

"Indeed she can, my Lady Marana. I have know many such. What is surprising is that Qala was able to reach the top so early and remain there." He chuckled. "Ambitious and ruthless. Just my sort of woman."

"But you most definitely are not her kind of man," spoke Saj. "Nor is anyone else."

"So it seems. I may try anyway."

"Xit likes a challenge," laughed Marana, her ill humor forgotten.

They were allowed the freedom of the pirate keep now, allowed to go anywhere on the Rock. Not beyond it. Not yet. At that moment, they stood on a rampart, gazing out across the great sea-fed lake that surrounded them. "Many of the pirates here choose to sleep on their ships," commented Saj. He pointed across the lake. "I am told there are barracks over there, too. Including ones for the galley slaves." He moved his hand to point a little further south. "And those are warehouses for the, um, booty. Also those slaves who are destined for market elsewhere." Nobles and rich merchants of his own home-land would buy some of those, to serve in their homes. Others might end up across the sea, or on Lorj, working the plantations there. Little slavery existed in Sharsh, though it was legal under the Muram regime.

"Much of their plunder never passes through here at all," he continued. "This is more of a safe haven than it is a center for the business of piracy."

"That was my understanding, too," said Xit. "This Qala does not so much rule as coordinate."

"And receives tribute from the ships, rather than a share. That way, it does not matter whether or not they report their profits honestly. Each pays the same for being a part of the fleet." Saj consid-ered this a sound business model.

"She will send for us again," spoke Marana. "What am I to do

124

about her interest in me?" she asked. "I would never give myself to another man, Saj, but this is, well, different. I think it is, anyway."

"Different and the same," Xit proclaimed. "You may ultimately need to make a choice, my dear, or perhaps we will be gone before then."

"I would marry you first, my Saj. I know, we said we would complete this quest before speaking of such things. But I would not give myself to Qala before you."

"Hush, my Marana," he told her, taking the young woman in his arms. "You will need to make no such decision."

~

It was only Saj who was called to Qala the next day. The Pirate Queen went straight to the matter of Marana, after pouring a goblet of dark wine for each of them. It was slightly vinegary, Saj felt.

"You know that I am — well, interested in your companion Marana." Qala half-reclined on a rich, if slightly threadbare, divan. Saj could see mildew on its wooden legs where it met the stone floor. He only nodded in reply.

"I am no monster. I would not force anything on her. Well, maybe a life of slavery, but that is business, you know?" Qala giggled at her own dark humor, until she saw the stricken look on the young Mur's face. "Don't worry, boy. I won't sell your Marana.

"Indeed," she continued, "I believe she could play a part in my legacy here. I can not rule the pirates forever."

"You see her as a possible successor?" That seemed astonishing, at least on first consideration. Not that Marana would not make a good queen, thought Saj.

"No, Saj. I see you as a possible successor. You are wasted reading the weather in a stone, not that it is not a useful talent. You have brains. You are practical and have a head for business, yet you are bold. That is what is needed here.

"Jacef is not suited to the position, even if he thinks he is. In honesty," she admitted, with a rather chilling smile, "I may just have to slip a knife into him sometime as a cure for his ambition."

125

THE EYES OF THE WIND

"I have no great desire to be the Pirate King," Saj told her.

"Neither did I when it was thrust upon me. The job grows on one." Her eyes swept the modest room that served as her private quarters, before fixing again on Saj. "This is not much, what I have here, though I revel in the power I wield. Yes, I admit that." She seemed lost in her thoughts for a moment.

No, it was not much. Qala's lifestyle seemed decidedly simple. She herself did not seem the powerful ruler of a pirate kingdom. A small woman she was, dressed much like one of her followers, kilt, a loose sleeveless blouse. One ring, a small white diamond in it, shone on her left hand.

"But I have put aside quite a large amount of gold during my tenure as queen," she went on. "It is safe, far from here, and one day I shall retire to enjoy it. Perhaps soon." There was an unaccustomed wistful note in her voice.

"Well, enough about that," she said, suddenly all business. "Marana. An arrangement would benefit the both of you. You should think upon it, as should she."

Saj was unsure whether to speak what was on his mind. He debated it with himself for a few seconds, before blurting out, "Marana would never love you."

"Perhaps not, perhaps so. I am willing to find out." Then she softened. "Love is what we all want, isn't it, boy? Can you blame me for seeking it?

"I enjoy the company of men from time to time but I know that I could never love one. No, not as I would love a woman. I wait for that woman and amuse myself as I can until I find her."

Qala sat silently for nearly a minute before saying, "You may leave me now."

~

Thrice now Saj had held the Sea Stone, gazed into it, told the pirates of storms in the Great Sea, even spoke of a rich cargo ship he had spied. Should he feel guilt over this? It was part of the business here, as he was a part.

Pirates would plunder, after all.

Jacef himself took the three of them on a tour around the lake, while on one of his own regular inspections. The man has no inkling of what his queen intends for him, thought Saj, and he had no plan to enlighten the pirate. He did not really like Qala's second much. No, that was not so — he did not like him at all.

Nor most of the other pirates they met. Any one of them would cut his throat for profit and pleasure, he knew.

"These are the barracks for the rowers," Jacef announced, as their boat came alongside a low pier. A barn-like wooden structure lay where it met the swampy ground, a structure raised on piles.

There was one large room, a surprisingly tidy room, with pallets spread in rows on the wooden floor. Men, most in naught but loincloths, sat scattered on that floor or on low benches along the walls. Saj could see staples for the attachment of chains, here and there, on those walls but none of the men wore any. He was sure that was not always so.

"Their quarters are better than I might have, um, expected." he remarked.

"It would be foolish to mistreat or starve the rowers," Jacef told him. "They are too valuable and of more use to us healthy. So long as they work hard and do as told, they get by."

Yet Saj could see the scar of many a lash on the men's backs.

He felt Marana's hand, sudden, shaking, on his arm. "My brother," she hissed in his ear. "That is my brother." Saj followed her eyes to a tall, lean man. Despite the thick beard, he could see a resemblance to Hurrum.

And he had recognized his sister, surely. He looked at them for only a moment before hanging his head. He would expect only the worst for her here, thought Saj.

Jacef was in conference with an older man, possibly he who ran this barracks. A retired pirate — what Qala hoped to become, but not here!

The Pirate Queen's second returned to them, stroking his scraggly chin whiskers. As many Mura, the man's facial hair was sparse.

Saj himself did not have a heavy beard. Maybe he would try growing it out someday, but for now he continued to shave, when he could.

"Nothing really to see here," said Jacef. "Let's go."

Marana took one look back and followed the pirate out onto the dock.

23

"We must get Corad away with us when we go."

"Absolutely," agreed Xit. "Why attempt one impossible task when we can tackle two?"

"Do you like it so much here?" snapped Marana in return. "Would you prefer to loll about on this rock and service the queen? We know where you went last night."

Both Saj and Marana had a good idea why Xit had been absent from their room.

"Yes, I shared Qala's bed," Xit admitted. "It was a welcome diversion for her and, perhaps, took her mind off you for a while." The look he gave Marana was all seriousness. "She is quite smitten."

"So it seems," said Saj. "But she can only be disappointed, in the end. I think even she knows that."

"Undoubtedly. Qala expects to be disappointed by life."

"She wants to retire, you know," Saj went on.

"Indeed? She mentioned nothing of this to me."

"So you are not as much her confidant as you think, eh?" asked Marana, with a rather satisfied look. Then she thought for a moment and added, "Maybe something can be made of that."

"Maybe so," agreed Xit. "I may hint of such things to her." He turned toward Saj. "It would seem though, that our Saj is the one in whom she confides. I wonder why?"

"Marana, in part," answered the Mur. "She knows we come as a set." Marana smiled at that. "But also, she, well, suggested I might consider being her successor."

Xit did not seem at all surprised. "An excellent choice, if you wanted the responsibility. You don't, do you?"

"No, he doesn't," spoke up Marana. "He is going to Lorj, where he will build me a tall house."

"That is so," agreed Saj. "Yes, that is so."

~

Saj sought. It was becoming almost effortless now to peer into the emerald Eye, the Sea Stone, and seek across future seas. Could I see what will be on land as well? he wondered. Saj suspected it would be possible, with some practice, but the gem was attuned to the water.

Storms. He often saw storms, and knew where to look for them at this time of year. Come summer, were he still among the pirates, he would need to search southward for the cyclones of the tropics. But now, they came from the north, rolling off Clisidon's coasts or down through the straits that separated that continent from the Muram peninsula.

He sought ships, as well. Sometimes it was the ships of the pirates themselves for which he looked, so he could report where they were, where they would be headed, whether, for that matter, they would remain afloat. This was of more importance and interest to his masters — and they remained his masters, no matter how high he might rise in Qala's esteem — than cargo ships they might plunder. They tended to know when and where those would be on the Great Sea, informed by the spies that operated in every port.

Saj let images slip into his mind unbidden for a few minutes. Most were meaningless, beaches, waves, sea birds. He saw little boats coming and going at Indabas, and at the mouth of the Chas, fishermen and the like who were of no interest to the pirates. And there, further up the Chas, galleys. That must be Azer where they docked. Or would dock; he sometimes forgot that these pictures were of things to come.

And how far in the future could be guesswork. He managed to come close when it came to the weather forecasts, most of the time. Apparently, he was more accurate than the late Agos so the pirates made no complaints.

Who stood, distant, dim, on that galley's deck? A tall figure, in a toga. The picture shimmered, dissolved. But he knew who it was — Hurrum, Marana's father.

He would come hunting them. That was why he was aboard that ship. Should Saj say something to the pirates, to Qala? He and his friends were caught between two threats and he was not sure which he should fear the more.

Nothing to do but wait and see what came. He recognized that this might present them with a possibility of escape. But it might be like the fish who escaped the heron by jumping into the mouth of the crocodile.

~

"Your wizard is schooled in many kinds of magic," Qala announced to Saj.

Xit smiled at this. "But it is not enough, is it, my queen?"

"No. No, it is not. Will anything ever be?"

Neither man had a ready answer for that. She had called both her wizards to her, once again in her private room.

Qala stood by her open window. She had a good window, a large window, that gave her a view of the channel leading into the lake. There were other channels, but they did not lead directly to the sea nor permit the passage of large vessels.

She watched a ship enter that channel, its oars rising and falling rhythmically.

"And I do not know if it matters," she spat out, her fists clenched in seeming rage and frustration.

"You are very angry, Qala. Is there a reason?"

"Just being alive is reason enough to be angry," she said, still staring out the window.

Xit shrugged at this. "I could be angry that nothing matters, except it doesn't matter."

"Ha, very true! I think I need to keep you, Xit, if only to make me laugh now and then." Qala did just that, then, but without much enjoyment. "Court jester for the Pirate Queen!" she proclaimed.

"It would be good to have a position."

"There are those who think your place should be at an oar. You do not do much around here, my little wizard, other than amuse me. And that too, I fear, will fade someday."

Qala sighed, very deeply. "All things fade," she told them. "I thought I had found love, once. Maybe I did." She held up the ring she wore on her left hand. "This was given me by one who was mistress of the man who ruled before me. He slew her in a jealous rage. And then I slew him. Yes, in a fair fight, sword against sword, I slew him. But it did not bring my beloved back to me.

"In less than a fortnight, it did bring me the power I still hold. There were others who would have ruled, had they been able. They were not able." She looked once again from the window, then turned back to her guests.

"The fools out there," she waved an arm more or less toward the mainland, "like to believe there is a point to things. They live their little lives, believing in their little gods. But we all end up the same. We all end up alone."

"That is only human, Qala. Humans are complex and so they crave simplicity. It anchors what is unmoored within them, allows the imposition of order where there is none. But, too readily, they become rigid in their politics, their personal beliefs." Xit allowed her to think on those words for a few seconds before going on.

"It is inevitable that we seek this order in our lives. I believe we would do best to recognize it for what it is. There must be a balance between becoming doctrinaire and denying all meaning."

"I am not at all sure there is any meaning. Even what I have here is naught, a flicker of flame in the darkness," spoke Qala. "But never mind all that. I have these moods."

She came and sat down on her shabby divan. "You believe in things, do you not?" It was uncertain which she was addressing.

"I believe in myself," asserted Saj, "and in what I can see. Life — that is enough."

Xit's expression was rather indulgent. "It *is* enough, for some. Others need more."

"Why?"

"If we could answer that question, we could answer our own," replied Xit. "Why, indeed?" He turned back to Qala. "I think you will never be happy here, my queen. Elsewhere? Who can say?"

~

"I requested a little boat for us," Saj announced, as he entered the room. "We are trusted enough now, and favorites of Qala."

132

"To escape? That would never work," scoffed Marana.

"No, to paddle about on the lake — and spy things out that might prove useful. Moreover," he said, "I convinced Jacef to assign a man to row it and act as our personal slave. He was reluctant, true, but I convinced him that you had become Qala's lover." Saj looked from Xit to Marana. "Even though another has that honor at the moment. I promised to report useful, um, gossip to him. I guess I shall have to make up some.

"Ha, I am talking in circles rather than getting to what I intended. Meet our new personal slave." He cracked the door and waved someone in. "I chose him myself."

"Corad!" Marana ran into her brother's arms.

The man seemed bewildered. "You are not slaves here?" he asked. "Not captives?"

"We talked our way out of that," Xit told him. "We are great talkers. Fighters, not so much." He gave the Sharshite a good look up and down. "We need to burn that loincloth and find you a razor."

"And then I will tell you our story," said Marana, glancing up to look at Saj, "Every bit of it."

~

Xit settled onto a stone bench along the ramparts. "It is time I spoke truthfully about myself," he began. "You have discerned who and what I am by now, though you have been discreet about it. Yes, I am Trickster. I can change my skin. I could become you, Marana, and take your place, seduce Qala.

"When I become a man, I wholly am a man, in every sense, with all man's limitations and mortality. If I became a woman — well, I might not want to be with Qala any more than you. Any attraction I feel for her now could easily melt away. Probably *would* melt away." He sighed and gazed out over the water. "And I have no idea how we would explain two Maranas. Perhaps I should just change back to a crocodile and swim away."

"Or eat her," suggested the girl. "I've heard of crocodiles eating pirates."

"She's barely a mouthful." Xit seemed lost in his own thoughts for some time. "It was a simple, thoughtless life, being a crocodile. But who I truly am would ever draw me back to my own world, eventually, until I again felt the desire to walk among mankind.

"As to Qala, I like her too much to eat her. I recognize she is dangerous, especially when she enters one of her black moods. Others like her I have known, full of energy one day, ready to throw themselves over a ledge the next." He chuckled. "Or throw us over a ledge."

He himself turned and looked over the ledge behind him. "She may be our best hope for leaving here with both our own lives and the Sea Stone."

Corad sat quietly on the stone floor at a short distance from them, playing the role of slave. An iron collar remained around his neck, an emblem of his status. He is listening to this all, thought Saj, but what thoughts does he have?

I should speak of his father. "I have seen the Thegn Hurrum," he stated in a low voice. "He has boarded a galley to come after us. Or soon will." He decided that information would be enough. Let them think on it.

24.

"You are the only one I trust to hear my words, boy."

"Not Xit?" Saj asked. "He would never betray you."

"No, but he might try to use me. Xit would put his friends and himself first." Saj had to nod in agreement; it was probably so. "He is the one who planted these seeds in my mind but I more trust you to pluck the fruit."

"You plan to leave," said the young man.

"Yes. It is time. I have no illusions that I would be allowed to go nor allowed to live if I voiced a desire. Jacef and others would see it as weakness and pull me down in their desire to replace me."

"Can't you simply board one of your galleys and sail away?" That seemed straightforward enough to Saj.

"I own no galleys and none of the captains would give me passage away. As soon as they saw what I was about, they would turn around and sell me to my enemies. No," she continued, "it would have to be one of the smaller boats I operate here in the lake or patrolling the coast. One such as that which found you on the beaches."

"I suspect that their crews would not be trustworthy, either," offered Saj.

"Not a chance," said the pirate. "Would you like some wine? Let us sit by the window."

Saj took a seat, a simple solid wood chair — cypress, he recognized — and gazed out the window until Qala brought mismatched goblets and sat too, sipping for a while before she again spoke.

"I am not watched but it would seem odd if I sailed away in one of those boats. I might conceal myself but who would serve as crew? You *are* watched and could not get away."

Qala said no more for some time, as both drank. A better wine, this time. Maybe new booty from some ship or another. Then, softly, she said, "Remember my offer to make you my successor remains. You and I and Marana could be happy together for two or three years before you let me slip away. And Marana might or might not choose to go with me."

No mention of Xit? "I do not believe Marana would ever agree to it."

He did not think she would, anyway. And what if Qala tired of one or both of them before then or became jealous if Marana chose him? No, she might mean it now but Saj did not know if the Pirate Queen could be trusted.

"Neither do I. But I thought I should try again, and remind you of that choice." Qala rose. "We must speak more on this later. Think on how we might proceed."

"I shall, Qala," he promised. Saj had many ideas; however, he felt it best he not mention Hurrum's ship to her.

~

"I dreamed last night," announced Saj. "I dreamed of all four Eyes and each was held by a young man." He directed his next words toward Marana. "They were our sons.

"The stones are not meant to go to the priests of Munu. I am sure I am to keep them and pass them on."

Xit nodded. "I believe the same, which is the reason I have traveled with you from the start. After all, you promised only to find and gather the stones. You never took oath to deliver them to Kambak."

"You noticed that, did you? It is somewhat second nature to me not to promise too much in a contract. Anyway, I have seen that I possess them in my future. Well, not quite *my* future, you know."

"But a future you shaped."

"Exactly."

"How will we know which son gets which gem?" asked Marana. She thought it a logical and practical question. "And will they have your gifts?"

"I think not," said Saj in reply to the second question. "As to their assignments, I have no idea. We'll find out, I suppose!"

"Let them choose," advised Xit. "When they are grown men, let them choose. They will know which is theirs."

"And what of our daughters?" asked Marana. "We are going to have daughters, too, you realize."

"I have not seen them, but I will take your word for it, my Marana."

~

Nighttime? Slipping out of the lake under cover of darkness would be the best choice. But there were patrols to prevent such things. Slaves occasionally bolted for freedom, stole a boat. All were captured. All were flogged. None survived that flogging.

Five refugees, their original three plus Corad and Qala. It would not take a very large boat for that. Even one the size that had brought them to the sea could work, if they chose to make their escape through the swamps.

That was the most important question, Saj felt. Whether to go out the main channel and make a dash in the open sea or to take one of the smaller ways and then either eventually find their way to the Great Sea or choose to go deeper into the swamps. One could be lost in there forever. But pursuit would be less of a problem.

And there were always watchers along the main channel, and many traps prepared against any enemy who might discover the way in. To go that way held no guarantee of reaching the sea at all.

The Mur preferred the idea of using the smaller channels, as larger boats would be unable to follow them there. Yet there were an abundance of smaller vessels that could. If only there were some way to send them the wrong direction!

Yes. That was it. Saj knew what he wanted to do. He had a plan. Now he need convince the others.

~

"I hope you are the only crocodile in this lake," whispered Saj.

"I would worry more about the poisonous water serpents," came Xit's jovial reply.

The two men stroked the inky waters, on either side of a boat of modest size. The moon was new and, moreover, clouds filled the sky. None would see them; they could see little themselves. The pair guided the vessel well out from the shore where it had been moored, and away from any ships anchored in this haven of pirates.

"This is far enough," felt Xit. "Let's start." Each had an auger. Hole after hole they drilled in the boat's bottom and sides until it was too low in the water to drill more. It had already floated low from several rocks they had placed inside.

That should do. It disappeared beneath the surface as they swam back toward the Rock.

"Now we hide," said Saj as they pulled themselves onto shore, away from the lights that always burnt on the quay.

Qala had chosen this spot for them to conceal themselves. Saj and Xit joined Marana and Corad in a cellar of sorts, a storage room seldom used due to the persistent leakage of lake water. Its floor was, in fact, lower than the lake's surface. The door, usually kept locked, was outside the keep, near the docks, where it would be easier to come and go unseen. In they slipped.

"What a reek!" The little store room stank of rotting vegetation. Water sloshed around Saj's ankles and he remembered Xit's remark about snakes. As soon as he found the place where Marana perched on some sort of table, he joined her. It, too, was dank and slippery, but better than the floor.

"Now it's up to this Qala?" came Corad's subdued voice. "Should we trust her?"

"We wouldn't have gotten this far if she intended to betray us," replied his sister. "She could have put a stop to the whole thing before we started."

"And she did give us weapons," added Xit. A sword for each of them, including Magpie's blade, which had rested in the Pirate Queen's own chambers for the past few weeks.

The only thing that worried Saj now was that Qala might not bring the Sea Stone with her when they finally took their leave of the Rock. He had done his best to impress on her the need for it, as a way to see if their enemies pursued them.

Without the Eye, all of this was for naught.

Dawn brought the sound of alarms, of men running back and forth outside, of boats being launched. "Take the boats out the channel and search both ways, up and down the coast," they could hear Qala order. All according to plan, so far.

But they would have to endure an entire day in here before they attempted to escape in earnest.

~

It was barely past sunset when Qala appeared at the doorway. Yes, she carried the cup and handed it to Saj without word. The pirate gestured for them to follow her.

"It is the best boat here," she told them, stopping by a trim little craft, practically a miniature galley. "Get aboard. We'll go out through the south passage and into the swamps."

"Will you, traitor?" There stood Jacef, sword in hand. With him were, what, two pirates? Yes. It was very dark, and difficult to make them out.

"I saw you bring this boat here and wondered about it. So you meant to run away with your girlfriend, did you?"

Qala's only answer was to draw her curved sword and lunge at the man. The pirates with him rushed past the battling pair to attack those at the boat.

We'll have to finish this quickly, Saj told himself, or more will come running. He clumsily parried a whistling swing of his attacker's blade.

Corad had the sword of Magpie in his hand and Corad was a man who had been trained in warfare. He took down his opponent almost immediately and turned to the man facing Saj. That man hesitated — a moment too long, as it turned out, for Xit had circled behind him in the concealing night and now thrust a knife between his ribs. Shouts arose from somewhere; lights bobbed in the distance.

And Qala and Jacef battled on, the slight woman, the tall man.

"Help her," called Marana from the boat. Saj knew if he did, the former queen of pirates would not forgive him. He reached out a hand to keep Corad from moving forward.

"Give her a chance," he said.

Qala was agile. She had been a far better fighter than her opponent, once, but she was no longer that young, active swordswoman who had claimed leadership here. Even so, none of those who watched the match would have had any desire to ever take her on. She needed to get inside Jacef's reach, get inside long enough to be effective with her blade. Once she slashed his leg; perhaps that would slow him down, in time, but there was no time.

Corad suddenly leaped up, swinging his sword violently in the air. The pirates eyes, for only a second, flickered as they were drawn to the distraction. In that second, Qala's sword came under his guard and into his chest.

"She'll never know," whispered Corad.

"I certainly won't tell her," responded Saj.

They shoved the boat out onto the lake and began rowing. But torches already shined at the water's edge. They knew pirates — those who remained at the base — were boarding their own boats to pursue them. The plan had been to cross the lake and enter one of the southern channels that would take them quickly into the swamp. That plan needed to be changed.

"Where's the closest channel?" yelled Saj. Qala pointed and they put their backs into the rowing.

"I thought I was done with this sort of thing," gasped Corad.

In a few minutes they were entering the passage, a bit of greater blackness in the night, closed in by thick mangrove. There were boats out on the lake now, torches flaring as they searched for the refugees. But those refugees were safe, hidden in the darkness of night and swamp.

25

"We could attempt to traverse these swamps and reach the Chas," said Saj. "That is how we came so we know it is possible."

Dawn's light was filtering through the trees. "Can you see any pursuit with the stone?" asked Qala. "That is why we brought it, isn't it?"

"In part." He looked to his companions. "Should we give her the story?"

"Later," said Marana. "But she's right. You should take a look in the Sea Stone."

"Sea Stone?" Qala had not before heard it named so.

"That's part of the story," said Saj, removing the platinum goblet from his bag. "I can feel the others. They have not been this close together before."

Marana looked toward Xit. "Could he see more if he had all of them in front of him?"

"Too dangerous. He has a bit of a rapport with this one now. Let's stay with it." He chuckled softly. "It might be dangerous for me, too."

Saj focused on the gem. Would it be even more potent if it were pried out of this cup? He suddenly felt that it would, though he was not sure why. He pulled out his dagger — Qala had made certain they were fully equipped with weapons — and began to bend back the retainers. There — and there. The stone fell into his hand.

Yes. It was free now. The power could flow more fully. He saw a boat speeding northward, toward a fleet, a pirate fleet. Ah, it was going to tell them of what had happened at the Rock. The pirates would be looking elsewhere for them now. That might be for the good if they chose to run for the sea.

Anything else? Another fleet? Muram navy. Maybe Hurrum was on one of those galleys. Or would be. He had to keep reminding himself these were things to come.

He would just as soon stay clear of both fleets. "Word will be spread to those who went searching for us," he told the others. "There will be boats combing the swamps." He had seen that, yes.

"It would be guessed we would head north," spoke Qala. "As we have."

"You could have told me we were headed any direction," replied Marana. All ways looked the same here. Nor did Saj have the pull of the Sea Stone to lead him, as it had when they sought the pirate base.

The flow of the black water could not guide them here, either. They were too far from the Chas for its current to have any effect. Only the rarely glimpsed sun gave them some indication of their heading. "Um, that would be north, right?" he said, pointing in what he thought the proper direction. "Then the sea is over there. We don't want to go that way."

"Not yet," agreed Xit. "It may become necessary."

"I say go east, further into the swamp." Saj saw himself as the leader here, and knew the others did, as well, but he wanted their approval on this. "At least for now."

Two days later, Saj suspected they were very near where they had started. They were days spent following twisting waterways among the cypress, dead ends, retracings. A great black and white woodpecker laughed at them from high in the trees. "We had best find a larger channel and follow it," he said.

"Do you think our pursuers have given up by now?" wondered Marana.

Qala shook her head. "They will not. Even if they withdraw from the swamps, there will be boats patrolling the coast. More boats than normal; there are always some."

"We could just hide until they give up," the Sharshite girl suggested.

"We would starve first, I think," spoke Xit.

"If the insects didn't eat us before then," added Corad.

"It is too bad you do not have your sling, Saj," Marana said. There was a frustration in her voice, restrained but there. "You could have knocked down a bird or something."

In answer, he pulled one out. "They are easy enough to make. I put this one together last night. But I have no pellets." He looked around and shrugged. "No rocks here. Nothing but mud."

"Unless you use one of those Marana has hidden away," jested Xit.

The girl laughed. "If I get hungry enough I may just give him one!"

~

So it was they rowed westward and did indeed find a wider channel, one with a definite flow. Perhaps it is only the tide, thought Saj, and it will flow the opposite way in a few hours. The water was somewhat salty when he dipped a finger and tasted it. Never mind; it was a way and they would take it.

Before any realized it, they had entered a small bay. They were nearer the Great Sea than Saj had thought. Surely that was a pass to the open water over there — a pass they should not attempt, as much as they wished to be away from the swamps. And there, entering the bay from the opposite end, was a pirate boat.

"To the sea," yelled Saj, and laid into his oar. It would be their only chance. The other boat immediately turned to follow, perhaps even intercept, their own. Four men could be seen in the vessel. Four men who fought and killed as a matter of their everyday occupation. His five, two of them women, could not hope to fight and survive.

But row they could, and this was a good boat, a fast boat, as Qala had promised. The former pirate leader was scrambling to get a sail aloft. That would give them the advantage they needed. She is good at this, isn't she? he thought. Cool and skillful. The striped triangular sail, white and black, billowed in the wind and they sped away from their pursuers, through the inlet and into the open sea.

The wind was not favorable for a northern passage, but they could manage. As long as there was no other pursuit, they could manage. An oar-driven galley would have no trouble overtaking them.

"They will be signaling the others," Qala announced in an even voice. "There will be pursuit."

"Flags?" asked Corad. He had observed the pirates' methods close-up for three years.

She but nodded in reply.

"They would have to be close already, would they not?"

"I am sure they are. It is how I would have positioned them."

Saj looked up. It was yet morning. If any ships came after them, they could not hope to escape into night. By noon, black sails could be seen and they drew steadily closer. Soon he could make them out — two galleys and nearly a dozen smaller craft pursued them.

There was no hope. Saj knew that. What of his visions of the future? Had they been but phantasms, might-have-beens? No, he knew he would reach Lorj and make his fortune there. It would be.

But there might be a detour. He continued to pull on his oar with all his strength, as did all but Qala, who minded the sail. Of a sudden, she shouted, "Ships ahead!"

Saj turned his head. Another fleet? But not pirates. He knew these were the ships he had seen when he gazed into the Sea Stone, the Muram fleet. Marana's father might be over there. Whether that was at all a good thing, he was uncertain.

But pirates most definitely were not. The ships quickly closed on them, a north wind filling their sails. There was a galley of the typical pattern, much like those that pursued them, and a pair of swift lighter vessels, such as were often favored by the pirates themselves. But in the center of this small Muram fleet was a great trireme, its three rows of oars rising and falling as it bore down upon them.

They steered to the side of the galley, the closest ship, and hands helped them up and onto the fore-deck. "Cutting it close there," came from the sailors and, "Bet you were glad to see us," and someone laughed and asked, "What did you do to get them mad?"

"Hold those men," came an icy voice. They turned to see the tall form of Thegn Hurrum.

Corad stepped forward. "Father."

"My son!"

~

The fleets were unequal in size and one might, at first, give the more numerous pirates the advantage. But the Mura had that trireme, a vessel more massive than any of the enemy ships. It could smash through any craft that got in its way, its heavy 'beak' crushing their hulls.

And it was fast, propelled by those three banks of oars, but not so maneuverable. Moreover, some of the smaller pirate vessels had the new, more efficient, triangular sails. In this close fighting, where oars trumped sails, that was not so much of an edge.

They were exceedingly useful, however, when the pirates turned and ran. They did that soon enough, once the trireme crashed into one of the lighter galleys, practically shearing it in two. The smaller boats that had been harrying the Muram vessels decided that was a signal to retreat and the remaining galley quickly followed. Its crew had been exchanging arrows with the galley on which the companions waited, unsure whether they were prisoners or guests.

There remained the broken galley and those aboard, abandoned by their fellows. "That's pirates for you," spat a sailor. "No loyalty to their comrades."

"But brains enough to cut their losses," whispered Qala, probably as much for herself as anyone else. It was just what she would have done, Saj suspected.

"It doesn't look like they are going to pursue," said Xit. "The trireme is too busy."

A contingent of Muram marines were swarming aboard the broken pirate galley, across boarding bridges they had thrown down, the iron-hooked ends fastening into the enemy vessel's decking. Fighting was hand to hand against the survivors, as the whole vessel slowly listed and began to sank. "Won't anyone free the rowers?" asked Marana, very quietly.

"It is unlikely," replied Qala.

Indeed, very few survived from that galley, pirate or slave. Those few who were captured were summarily hung from the flagship's mast. They could be seen kicking as they struggled to hold onto life for a minute or two more.

"It's better than being crucified if they were taken back as captives," whispered Xit.

Saj looked to those bodies, swaying with the rolling of the

145

trireme, and then quickly away. He could only hope he wouldn't be joining them.

SETTING VI.
SETTING SAIL

26.

At last, attention was turned to the five refugees, who had remained seated on the deck through the fight. They rose as the captain of the vessel approached, Hurrum at his side. He won't be the admiral of this fleet, felt Saj. That individual would be on the biggest ship, the trireme. They would face another interview with him, if they survived this one.

The thegn turned a suspicious eye on Qala.

"Do not betray her, Brother, I beg you," whispered Marana.

"This woman was a fellow prisoner," spoke Corad. "And these two," he swept an arm toward Saj and Xit, "are my comrades."

The noble Sharshite gave that pair a very long look and then addressed Saj. "You slew Lord Gawif," he stated.

"I did, sir," admitted the young Mur.

"Hmm, it turns out that was a good thing. When his papers were examined, it was found that he was in league with the Pretender."

Marana smiled at that and gave Saj a knowing look, which Hurrum caught. "You knew this?"

"We were at the Pretender's court, my lord," explained Saj.

"Yes, of course, I knew that. And you stole his jewels while you were there." The man shook his head. "It wasn't bad enough for you to read romances, Marana. You had to be in one!

"And you have brought my son back to me. My heir." He cocked his head at Marana. "That lets you off the hook, my girl, as far as providing more of them for me goes. We shall speak further of this later. But now," he said, turning to Corad, "I have much to discuss with this lost son of mine."

They walked away, the father's arm around the son. "It would seem our lord Hurrum is not going to ask for your blood, nor any other parts of you," drawled the captain, a man of Sharsh. "I have my suspicions about you, madame," he said to Qala, "but there are others who will wish to sort that out later. For now, you have the freedom of my ship." He turned to his second officer. "See to quarters for these folk."

"Pallets on deck will do," Xit said.

Marana, however, had something else to ask. "Tell me, Captain," said she, "can you marry people?"

~

They were given not pallets but, rather, a small room — possibly a quickly-cleared storeroom. Marana, it was assumed, would occupy her father's cabin, as would Corad. "I would rather stay with my compan-ions," she told the officer. The man only shrugged. It was of no matter to him.

"I am quite peeved at that captain," spoke Marana, "refusing to marry us without Father's permission." She did not sound at all serious about it.

"Then you must simply obtain his permission," Xit told her.

"You have mentioned other gems," spoke Qala.

Xit chuckled. "Eager to hear the story?" He turned to Marana. "Why don't you show her?" That he backed off a bit as she reached into the pouch hidden in her clothes, no one failed to note.

One by one, she laid the Eyes of the Wind before her on a blanket. "The last one," she said to Saj, holding out her hand. He passed the Sea Stone to her without word and she placed it with the others.

"The Earth Stone," said Marana, indicating the golden jewel. "Fire Stone. Sky Stone," she continued, pointing each out. "And now, the Sea Stone." She looked up at Saj. "Your quest is complete." She smiled and shook her head. "No, our quest."

Saj barely heard her. He stared at the four jewels for a few seconds and then, as Xit, backed away. "A bit much, aren't they?" whispered the little wizard.

148

Marana gathered all four and tucked them away again. "Let me tell you of them, Qala." She glanced at Saj, perhaps seeking his approval before beginning.

"You are a better storyteller than I," he told her. "Go ahead."

"So what do you do with these Eyes now?" asked the former pirate, at the end of the tale. "They could command a high price." Was there a glitter of avarice in Qala's eye?

"They come with us to Lorj," Saj stated. "There is no question of this."

"Too bad," said Qala.

~

A broad-shouldered, bandy-legged Mur clambered up a rope and onto the galley. Most of his outfit seemed little different from that of the common sailors here, but Saj could recognize that he was of high rank by the broad sash about his middle. Swords hung at both sides, one long, the other short and curved.

"The admiral, I would wager."

"And you would win," replied Xit. "Not that I would ever expect you to lay a wager, friend Saj. It's not in you to be a gambler."

Unless one considered this whole adventure one great gamble, Saj told himself. The man walked over to them, his gate rolling.

"Lord Hurrum joined our expedition with plans to hunt you down, boy, and award you a painful death," he stated, with no prelim-inaries. "It seems he has changed his mind. It's all the same to me." A shrug, perhaps exaggerated, with palms spread out. "But I would rather have not delivered a good Muram lad like you to him for the crime of being in love. That is the girl?" he asked, looking past him at Qala.

"No, Lord Admiral," said Marana, stepping forward. She could hear the former Pirate Queen snicker behind her. "That would be me."

"Oh, of course. My eyesight is not so good anymore." He turned to Saj. "Tall, isn't she?"

"I would not want an inch less of her."

"Maybe you could marry us," suggested the girl.

The Muram sailor laughed. "Ha, your father warned me you might ask. No, my dear, the thegn has other plans for you."

He saw the sudden consternation on both their faces, poor eyesight or not. "Fear not, lovebirds. You need not make another run for it nor think he will separate you. Hurrum seems resigned to your match." He beamed benignly upon the couple. "And to having an heroic son-in-law."

"I am only a man of business," objected Saj.

"I believe that," returned the admiral. "But circumstances can make any man a hero." He looked again at Qala, squinting his eyes. "Then who is that lovely creature?"

"A fellow captive," explained Marana, "forced to work as scullery maid in the pirates' kitchens." Saj suspected Qala was having trouble keeping herself from laughing again.

"Ah, the poor lass. I must speak further with her later. She might have, um, useful information."

Good luck getting anything more from her, thought Saj.

~

"What am I to do with you?" asked the thegn. He had called them to his cabin; his son, Corad, sat quietly on a chest in the corner.

Which he was addressing was uncertain. Perhaps both. But it was Saj who spoke. "You need do nothing, my lord. We were on our way to Lorj and shall continue that journey."

"Ha, bold talk, merchant! But we are going the opposite direction now." The fleet had turned north, returning to harbor in the River Chas. The wind was unfavorable, progress slow, but they would get there.

"There are outward bound ships in Azer, Father," Marana informed him.

"Yes, there are. Saj here should definitely take one of them. But you, Marana." The nobleman shook his head. "It is not the match I would have chosen. It is not even near the match I would have chosen. But you two have adventured together nearly a year. Are you, well —"

"Lovers, Father? We promised not to even consider such things until Saj finished his quest."

"A quest. You have spoken of this before but I know not what you mean by it." He glanced at Corad. "I assume your brother does and that you will explain it to me, eventually. But this traveling you two did — if you say naught happened between you, I shall believe, Marana. But any prospective husband I might have chosen probably would not."

Corad spoke. "You could not find a better one than Saj, anyway. I would gladly call him Brother."

Saj thanked the man silently. "We shall have time to discuss this further," said Hurrum. "On dry land."

~

"It doesn't hurt to be on Murgie's good side," reasoned Qala, "and he is diverting." By 'Murgie,' she meant Admiral Murgom. Qala had spent much time in his cabin lately. Now she stood on the broad deck of the trireme with Saj and Xit, watching the coast slide by. Beneath their feet, they could hear the beat of a drum, keeping time for the rowers.

Xit scowled. Was the man — or whatever he actually was — jealous? "He is not your equal, Xit. Far from it. Why, you are almost as good as a woman." She giggled at that. "But after he hurries through what he mistakes for lovemaking, he tells the most entertaining stories."

"Quick, eh?"

"That's not such a bad thing. I would just as soon he get it over with."

Saj was glad Marana was not there. She would be as red as a woodpecker's cockade.

"And I suspect it will all be over with as soon as we dock at Azer." They had entered the Chas and would soon reach port. "The admiral keeps a mistress there — and she is welcome to him!"

"What will you do in Azer, Qala?" asked Saj. A change of topic would be all to the better, he felt.

151

"Look at everything!" she exclaimed. "It is long since I walked the streets of a city."

"Did you never leave the Rock?" That would have been a dreadful, boring existence indeed.

"Oh, no, boy. I got away every year or two for a little while. Mostly across the sea to the old kingdoms, to do business. Once to Matanas — horrible little place."

"But not as horrible a little place as the Rock, I would think," spoke Xit.

"At least I was boss there. I shall be nobody where we go. I do not regret it, though. Not one bit." Her smile seemed forced. "But maybe we are all nobodies anyway, in the end. My life still seems without any point."

Xit spoke more gravely than was his wont. "We are but infinitesimal specks in the cosmos. Yet each of us is as important as any other infinitesimal speck. Beyond that, there is little to be said."

"Perhaps not, friend Xit. I hope they have good shops in Azer. Wasting money is as effective a means as any to stave off melancholy."

27

Up the broad Chas the ships rowed. Saj and Xit — and pretty much everyone except Marana — felt it was wise for the pair and Qala to finish their journey on the admiral's flagship, separate from Hurrum and his family. They would speak again with the thegn soon enough.

Azer appeared on the northern banks, first a few isolated shacks and warehouses, then more, closer together, larger buildings along the shore, docks, a squat fortress tower in the Muram style. It was a large town, Saj could see, though not near the equal of Indabas. That might change some day, if the valley of River Chas became more heavily populated, more prosperous. To their right, the southern side, the land was all marsh, though a few structures rose here and there on pilings.

"Over there," said Xit, gazing toward one of the docks lining the waterfront. "They'll be coming to see us, sooner or later."

A group of saffron-robed men, perhaps a dozen all told, stood watching the ship. The priests of Munu. "They know where we are, once again," remarked Saj.

"And again I would assume they have their spies and sources. But then, it is possible there is sorcery involved. None of those," he said, nodding in the direction of the priests, "but there may be those with gifts in their employ."

"They will learn soon enough that they will not get the Eyes. Where do they dock this monster of a ship?"

"I would guess it will remained anchored in the river. But didn't we pass a shipyard back that way?" Xit gestured downriver.

"We did. If it needed hauling out, I reckon that's where they would do it."

"Most likely," agreed the little wizard. "But this ship would not have been built there."

No, it wouldn't. Probably laid up in his own homeland, thought Saj. "We have come to a stop." The oars were being drawn in. Would those rowers, slaves all, sleep in the cramped space where they worked? The Muram navy did not treat those who rowed their ships nearly so well as did the pirates.

But their supply was nearly unlimited as long as they warred, as long as men were condemned to this punishment by harsh laws. It was a system that could not last. Yet another reason to get away, take Marana to Lorj, and build a life there, far away.

"There goes the anchor," he said. "I wonder how soon we can be ashore?"

~

"It seems that Qala and Admiral Murgom's mistress have become quite good friends," said Marana.

Saj yawned. He felt the need for a siesta on this mild day. It wasn't right that it should be this warm in winter. And it would be worse in Lorj, wouldn't it? "It will not be a lasting friendship," he answered. "Qala does not intend to stay in this town."

"No. They, um, entertain each other while Murgom visits the brothels. She is already looking into traveling away." Marana turned her eyes to the ships moored in the river. "We should soon do the same."

"That is so. Our quest is at an end." Saj turned to her and spoke. "So, my Lady Marana, I must ask: will you marry me?"

"Will you give me time to think about it? Qala's offer is still on the table."

"Only ten seconds." He began to count. "One. Two. Threeee. Foooouuuur."

"Very well, Saj of Muradon, I accept your proposal. We will marry and have, what, four sons you said?"

"That I saw," Saj answered. Probably there were no others. "I think two might have been twins."

"Ah, one less pregnancy then. That is welcome news."

"You do not wish to bear my beautiful children?"

"*Your* beautiful children?"

"Of course I shall proudly act as though it were all my doing."

"Of course. We must name one of our sons for my brother," Marana stated. "That is not open for discussion."

"Then we must name another for my brother, Borm," asserted Saj.

She wrinkled up her nose at that. "What? Saddle him with a barbaric Muram name?"

"Borm is a good name. A good man and a good brother, too."

"Is he like you?"

"In some ways, but about twice my size. He cracked some of my ribs one day in a playful wrestling match." He turned his eyes northward. "I have not seen him in two years and doubt I ever shall again. Borm was content to stay in our home village and ply the trade of carpenter."

"So there are big men in your family. I feared all our children would be of your size."

"And what is wrong with that? Should they all be as tall as your brother and as wide as mine?"

"That sounds good."

~

"A wedding at Sarowhem is out of the question," stated Hurrum. "But I shall see you two married before you go anywhere.

"I have dispatched messages to our home," he continued, speaking now to Marana, "and your mother will soon be on her way here."

The pair looked at each other. "Should we find a priest?" asked Saj. "What cult do you prefer?"

"I would have been content with being married at sea," the noblewoman replied.

"As long as his ship remains in the river, I think the admiral could do that."

The thegn shook his head. "I do not know if you children are being serious or are just pulling the tail of this old jackass. I shall arrange every thing. Or the Lady Belema will, as soon as she arrives."

Marana did not look overjoyed at this news. "The ceremony will be held at Captain Nedos's house," Hurrasu went on. "We are old friends, he and I."

If that were not so, there would have been no ships to rescue them, Saj knew. This Nedos was captain of the galley that had taken

155

them aboard and a member of the new lesser nobility under the Mura, a Patrician of the Empire.

"None of this matters that much," the thegn went on. "Married is married. More important is what happens after."

"Father!" scolded Marana. "We know all about that!"

The nobleman laughed uproariously. "No, no, Daughter. I meant what you would do with your lives. Where will you go? What will this Mur do to support you?" He looked Saj up and down. "I know he is a competent fellow but far from wealthy."

Near penniless, actually, Saj said to himself.

"But he has these," spoke Marana, taking the hidden pouch from her gown and laying the Eyes, one by one, on the table before them. "They are probably worth a small fortune as jewels but they have a greater value, as well. Let me tell you our tale."

~

Qala gave her mount a good looking over. "I hope it is gentle. I have not sat a horse in near twenty years."

"You could have had a litter, my lady," spoke the hostler.

She was dismissive of the idea. "Those are for old women. I intend to spend much time on horseback from now on and hope never again to even smell the sea."

"I wish you good luck with that," said Saj. "You have wealth, you said?"

"I own much property, upriver where none would know me. My agents have been buying it for me for many years." She looked to where the Thegn Hurrum stood speaking to some soldiers. "Your father and I shall almost be neighbors."

"I will pray to Esefa that you find someone there," Marana promised. "Someone for you."

Qala only raised an eyebrow at that. "Esefa? Would she care for one like me?"

"She is the goddess of all love," Marana maintained. "Surely she will bring it to you, as to others."

"Maybe so."

Marana embraced the former pirate warmly, before stepping back to scold her. "Hey, don't feel me up!"

"I had to get something out of all this," replied Qala. She mounted her pony and rode north.

"I think she got quite a bit out of it," Saj said. "And I think neither your father nor the admiral believed her to be an innocent."

"She could have guided a Muram fleet into the pirate stronghold," Marana replied, "which I think is truly why we were pursued. But, once again, choices have been made."

28.

"So, young man, we meet once again and once again you are going to steal something from me."

"I will not apologize for my coming theft, my Lady Belema, but I must for our last meeting. Circumstances beyond my control led to it."

"Your decisions, and those of my daughter, led to it. Well, no one was harmed and I would thank your bandit leader for that. What became of Lord Magpie?"

Lord Magpie? The outlaw would be turning over in his grave, if he had one. "He is dead, my lady."

"Oh, I am sorry to hear that. He was a gentleman."

"That he was, Lady Belema. That he was."

"Now I must look at Lord Nedos's hall. Is it big enough, Hurrum?" she asked her husband.

"You should not call him 'lord,'" he told her. "He is something a bit less than that. Why don't I take you to look at it?"

"What exactly is a patrician?" whispered Marana as they fell in behind her parents.

"A full citizen," explained Saj, who knew the ins and outs of Muram titles. "The equal of any upper-class Mur, able to bring lawsuits against any man and to petition the emperor. In essence," he finished, "Captain Nedos has become Muram."

"In some ways a more powerful title than my father's and, in some, a lesser one." She suddenly stopped and looked at her soon-to-be husband. "Are you considered an upper-class Mur?"

"Well — I am a Mur, in the original sense. The word meant nothing other than nobleman when the first of my ancestors rode into Clisidon across the sea, many centuries ago. Any of more or less pure blood came to be known as a Mur, to differentiate them from those they had conquered.

"And, in the sense it is used in the empire, now, I am of a patrician family. That does not mean we had any money or power, just that we were descended from those men who founded our nation. That makes me fully a citizen. It does not mean so much anymore, when things are controlled by powerful, wealthy men who own estates far from our homeland." His face soured. "Men who bought the name of patrician."

"Ah. So you are the equal of Nedos. That is good to know and I shall make certain Father is aware of it. Let's catch up."

The captain's hall was sufficient in all eyes except those of Belema. "No one much will be here," Marana reminded her mother. "My Saj has no family near."

"I consider Xit my brother," said the Mur. "There are no others."

"That makes your side of the invitations simple," observed Captain Nedos, joining them. "But I will add the admiral and, ah, his guest to it. He offered to stand in for your father." The sailor asked, "Deceased, isn't he?"

"He is." Saj saw no reason to elaborate.

Nedos nodded. "Mine as well." He, likewise, chose to add nothing more. "So this Xit can act as your second here, unless you prefer another. Lady Marana's brother, maybe?"

"Xit will do." One last adventure together, in a way, with the sorcerer once again at his side.

"I have engaged a priest of Jov," stated Hurrum. "Marana tells me he is your preferred divinity."

Saj had to laugh. "Any would have done, my Lord Hurrum. Any can speak the words we wish to hear."

~

The High Priest of Munu approached the three, there on the docks of Azer. The others of his order followed quietly behind him.

"We are ready to receive the stones," spoke Kambak. "You have done well, young sir."

Saj looked fully into the man's soft, dark face. "I have decided to keep the Eyes," he told him.

"You would break our bargain?"

"On the contrary. I never promised to give you the stones, only to gather them."

159

THE EYES OF THE WIND

Kambak screwed up his forehead in thought. Then he slowly nodded. "This is true. I bargained poorly. So what more do you wish? All we have is yours, and there is more on Lorj."

"I want only the Eyes of the Wind. I have seen that they are destined for me."

"We shall see about that," came the High Priest's curt reply. He turned and spoke to his followers in their native Baxac. Saj assumed that was what it was.

All twelve priests raised their staffs and began to chant. "We call upon the Spawn of Bakap!" thundered Kambak. He stood, gazing out upon the river for several seconds before saying, "It is done." The saffron-robed holy men turned and filed away.

"That is it?" asked Saj.

"It will take some time. Hours, maybe." Xit turned from the Chas. "Nothing to do but wait. Let's get some wine."

The three ducked into a nearby tavern, a place that catered to travelers and dockworkers alike, a place that was surprisingly airy, with large windows opening onto the docks. Three tumblers of wine soon were before them.

Saj sipped from his cup and spoke something that had been on his mind. "I've never understood why the priests want the stones."

"To create an oracle. Gathering all four Eyes at one place of power would grant visions unparalleled, even for seers of little natural talent." Xit drank deeply from his tumbler before going on. "Such a place of power as the mighty volcano of Kamazad in Lorj."

"Would that be a bad thing?" asked Marana.

Xit shrugged. "Perhaps not, if Saj had not seen a great cataclysm coming. Kamazad would not be a safe place for the Eyes." He leaned forward to speak earnestly to the two. "It is for you, and your heirs, to keep the stones safe."

Screams arose outside the tavern. "It has begun," said Xit. "We'd best go take a look." He gulped down the last of his wine before going to the docks.

A huge sea serpent reared above the River Chas, its mouth large enough to swallow the boats now rocking in the waves of its passage.

Mottled gray and green it was, with a long red tongue and wiry whiskers sprouting from its head. It was seeking something, moving that head back and forth.

Saj knew it sought him. "How?"

"Some sorcerer in Kambak's employ would have placed a geas upon it to come when called. The priest has no such powers himself," Xit explained.

Marana stared at the monster. "Is it the leviathan?" she wondered, in a very small voice.

"No, my dear," replied Xit. "I am the leviathan. That is the Bakawan, one of the children of Bagap, the great snake who dwells at the bottom of the sea." He looked out toward that enormous, menacing form. "And now I must leave you. Farewell, Marana. Farewell to you, my friend Saj." With that, the little man turned and leaped into the water.

"Xit!" cried Saj. "What is the fool doing?"

"Making his choice, Saj. Xit knows very much what he is doing."

A moment later, the Bakawan fixed its eye on Saj and began to swim toward him, great oar-like fins propelling the serpentine body.

The water boiled between them and the beast. Then, the largest crocodile they, and perhaps anyone else, had ever seen burst from the river. Straight up, like an arrow shot at the sun, it hurtled and its wide jaws closed on the serpent.

There was little to see but churning water as the two battled, their bulk obscured by the waves and foam. Some dark ichor stained that water.

"See him roll!" cried someone. "The crocodile will not release its grip!"

Then, nothing for long minutes. What was that? A piece of something bobbed to the surface, and another, mottled green and gray. Then the crocodile's massive head appeared. It seemed to stare, unblinking, toward the docks for a time before the creature turned and propelled its monstrous form down the Chas, toward the sea and out of their lives.

"Is he gone from us?" whispered Saj, loosening his arms from

161

around Marana. He had not realized how tightly he had been holding her.

"I think so," said Marana. "If Xit — or maybe I should call him Xido — truly becomes whatever form he takes, then he may think and act like a crocodile now. He will swim the seas until he wearies of this world and then return to wherever he comes from." That seemed to make sense to her. She hoped it did to Saj.

He nodded. "One of those infinite worlds of which he told us. Maybe, like the shadows he drew here, Xit was never entirely in this universe of ours."

"I think our quest has truly ended," she said.

"Then all that is left is for us to marry."

~

Hurrum looked the Eyes over. "So you insist on taking these with you to Lorj." A statement, not a question.

"I must," replied Saj. "I serve them, protect them, and they, I think, will serve me in turn." To Marana, he said, "Best tuck them away now. May we be in Lorj before I next look upon them."

"And you need to hurry to your mother," Hurrum told her. "I don't think you and Saj were supposed to see each other right now."

Away went Marana, to hide away the Jewels of the Elements and to don her wedding gown.

"I do wish the two of you would reconsider heading for Lorj. I know it is a place of promise, but might there not be dangers?"

"There may be pursuit to Lorj eventually, by any who might desire the Eyes. We do not know if Kambak and his order will leave things as they are. But I would deem it safe if we keep our heads low and do not reveal them to anyone. As safe as here."

"Maybe so, maybe not. Let's find your second," said the thegn.

That second, with the departure of Xit, was to be Hurrum's son. They found him huddled in the hall with Captain Nedos, conferring on something that might or might not be of importance. Hurrum addressed the pair. "Couldn't we talk this boy into remaining in Sharsh? There must be positions for him right here in this town."

"Lorj is not a bad place to start a new life," was the captain's opinion.

Corad took an opposing view. "If one is a criminal or bankrupt. Saj has family here now." To his father, he said. "He would make a good agent for your estates."

"He would, but he wants to be his own man."

"As would I," spoke Nedos. "When I am at sea, I answer to no one."

"Don't mention that to the admiral," Hurrum told him. "Well, boy," he said, "turning to Saj, "if you insist on Lorj, I will not stand in the way. But know that you would always be welcome to return. Preferably with grandchildren for me to spoil. You will head for Matanas?"

"That is our plan, sir, at least as a starting point."

"Forget Matanas as a place to settle," advised Nedos. "The plantation owners control things up there. Try one of the Ducal Cities or even Lanlaz."

"Lanlaz — that is a free city, isn't it?"

"Aye, with an elected Lord Mayor. As snug a harbor as any you would ever hope to sail into, as well."

Hadn't Saj seen a good harbor, almost a lake, in his dreams? Or was he confusing that with memories of the pirate's port? "That sounds like a proper place for us."

"I have contacts down there," admitted Hurrum. "They can help you get started."

"In Lanlaz, Father?" asked Corad.

"In Lanlaz, Son. Our agents have found it easier to deal with the merchants and planters there than the ones in Matanas. The bribes needed are much smaller!"

Captain Nedos laughed at that. "I can believe it." To Saj he said, "I will patrol as far as Matanas next month. I do not think Murgom would mind me taking a couple passengers along. You would want to go overland from there, I think."

"So, how long yet?" asked Corad. "I saw the priest arrive. Let's not give him time to get drunk."

"Not until sunset. Plenty of time for us to drink, as well, and fortify our young groom for the ceremony."

Saj held up a hand. "There is one other reason I wish to take the one I love to Lorj, and I think you three should know of it." He sighed. Was it right to speak of this? "I have seen an event to come, a terrible event, a time when the earth will shake and the seas will rise. I would not wish Marana in Sharsh when it comes, nor our children. It will be known to future generations as the Devastation.

"I think I shall no longer be young when it comes. I do know that my family will be safer, forewarned, in Lorj. And now I warn you."

"This is certain?" asked Hurrum. Saj but nodded. "If it is as you say it will be, I shall no doubt sit with my ancestors."

"But we will not." Corad glanced at the captain.

"If I sense that it is near, I shall attempt to send word," promised Saj.

"Will the empire end?" asked Nedos.

"I am not certain. I think not but its grasp will never be as great as now. Sharsh will slip from it."

Corad spoke. "Then so would Lorj."

"That is so." And his sons would be ready when it happened.

~

A bride, all in white, a flower chaplet on her head, approached Saj. A father, in spotless toga, accompanied her.

I think Corad is more nervous than I, thought the Mur, as he sensed the man shifting his weight back and forth behind him, like a cornered animal ready to bolt. You would think him the one getting married.

Ha, his father undoubtedly has a match in mind for him. Maybe he should bolt.

How did Lady Belema find so many flowers at this season? The hall overflowed with them. And here was his bride, beside him. Hurrum went to a seat between his wife and Admiral Murgom.

Murgom's mistress was on the other side of the sailor, and already crying.

The priest took his hand and Marana's, placed them together. How did the words go? "I shall be one with my wife. I shall be Marana," he said. Praise Jov his voice did not crack. And she, Marana, was pledging to be one with him, the little Muram trader who had wandered into her father's villa one day.

Saj could not see his own future, but it did not matter.

He knew it would be wonderful.

AFTERWORD

I hope you have enjoyed THE EYES OF THE WIND. This is my tenth novel, and is set in the world of my DONZALO'S DESTINY sequence, but thirteen or so centuries earlier. The technological level is meant to be similar to that of Late Antiquity or the very beginning of the Medieval period.

The magic, however, is the same. The novel serves as a sort of bridge between my Malvern books and the Donzalo ones, but it is not necessary to read any of those to understand this one. Of course, I hope you will!

It is possible that Saj will eventually play a leading role in another novel. And those sons of his — well, we shall see.

Stephen Brooke

Author Stephen Brooke lives in an old farmhouse in the Florida Panhandle. *The Eyes of the Wind* is his eighteenth book and tenth novel.

www.ingramcontent.com/pod-product-compliance
Lightning Source LLC
Chambersburg PA
CBHW032149020726
47496CB00003B/789